2 0

betrayal

BOOK 2

2099

betrayal

John Peel

BOOK 2

AN
APPLE
PAPERBACK

SCHOLASTIC INC.
New York Toronto London Auckland Sydney
Mexico City New Delhi Hong Kong

ISBN 0-439-06031-1

12 11 10 9 8 7 6 5 4 3 2 1 9/9 0 1 2 3 4/0

Printed in the U.S.A.

First Scholastic printing, November 1999

This is for Brian and Judy Heinz

Prologue

New York was dying, inch by inch, building by building.

Inspector Shimoda stared out the window of her apartment, watching what she could see of the collapse, and imagining more. She was high enough to be able to view hundreds of buildings — mostly residential, but some businesses. Lights were going out, and the buildings were turning gray and cold. Her own apartment was already dead, one of the first hit by the Doomsday Virus.

The virus had attacked the computers that kept New York alive and moving. It had ravaged those machines, ruining them completely. Anything it touched was destroyed. Then it leaped to some new machine to infect and annihilate. The results of this attack were becoming more and more apparent as the inspector watched.

It wasn't simply a matter of wiping out the controlling computer programs. It was clear that the program's creator had added a nasty little twist to it. Before the virus struck, other smaller viruses attacked the systems. They were obviously designed to cause safety mechanisms to break down. It was the only explanation for the flits continuing on their way once their power had been cut off. Brakes should have been applied, but weren't. People were dying in mangled wrecks.

The monster behind this disaster was clearly intending to inflict as much pain, suffering, and death as he could before he caused the fatal crash of the Net.

Beside Shimoda, the young thief known as Genia also stared out in horror. Genia prided herself on being a renegade computer genius, but even she was appalled at what was happening, and the speed at which it was occurring.

There were several fires already. Smoke hung over a dozen buildings, and in some cases Shimoda could see the flames. Her heart sank. With the computers dead, so many things could go wrong. One small spark, and rooms could catch ablaze. Security systems wouldn't work, and the automatic fire extinguishers were just so much junk without commands. All electronic lines were wiped, so people couldn't call for help. And, even if they could call, how could the fire department respond? Without computers, their vehicles wouldn't start, their equipment wouldn't work. . . .

Anyone caught in an on-fire building was doomed. The doors wouldn't open. The windows, of course, were unbreakable in high-rises, to prevent deaths (accidental or otherwise). Unless the inhabitants had opened their windows before the failure, the apartments would be sealed. People would be trapped and burned to death. . . .

Shimoda shuddered at the thought. So far, she and Genia were okay. But for how long? Nothing had gone wrong in her apartment, but they couldn't get out. And if a fire started anywhere in the building . . . She shuddered again. To be trapped in here, with no way out, burned to death . . . Or would they die of smoke inhalation first? Either way, a terrible way to perish.

And, anyway, even if she could get the door open, it would do no good. They were on the thirty-seventh floor. The elevators wouldn't be working. Shimoda realized suddenly that if anyone had been in an elevator when the virus had struck, they would have died as the cages plunged down the shafts. That was how the virus's creator had obviously planned it — all safety overrides were useless. There was absolutely no way for her to know how bad conditions were out in New York. But she suspected that, no matter how dreadful she imagined them to be, they were probably ten times worse. The monster behind this had an imagination that was only exceeded by his complete lack of moral scruples.

Even if she and Genia could escape from her apartment, there was no way to be sure they'd be safer anywhere else in this city under assault.

So much horror. So much pain. So many deaths. It was her job to stop them, to catch the person responsible for all of this mayhem. And there was *nothing* she could do. She was trapped here, powerless — quite literally. Without system power, none of her Terminals would work.

Except her wrist-comp, of course, which had its own power source.

Surprised that she hadn't remembered this before, the inspector triggered a signal. If she could call in Computer Control, perhaps someone there could do something. Send a special aircar, maybe. That was, *if* her link was still operative. With everything else that was happening, nothing was certain now.

The wrist-comp lit up to show it was operating, but there was no reply from the other end. Shimoda scowled. *What was happening?* Then she realized that there had to be thousands of calls streaming in for help. Hers was just one of many, and would be answered when there was someone free to do so. It could be a long wait. . . .

And all the time she was wasting standing here, the villain behind this savage and ghastly attack would be making his getaway. There would be no way for her to catch up with Tristan Connor after this.

But she would. She *had* to — they could not leave this attack on New York unpunished. Tristan Connor *must* be caught, publicly tried, and spectacularly dealt with. And, she vowed, she would be the one to bring him down.

Just as soon as she could escape from her own home . . .

1

Tristan Connor stood in the street, looking over the East River at New York City. He was badly shaken by the events of the last few hours, but physically pretty whole. It was mostly shock that he had to deal with. He had hardly had the time to adjust to the fact that he had been adopted by his parents as a baby, and that he wasn't their natural son. And now . . . now he had just been told that he was not only adopted, but that he was a clone. And, as if that were not enough, he was the clone of a sick and twisted individual named Devon, who had created and now unleashed the Doomsday

Virus on New York — if not the world. And who had then ordered his henchmen to kill Tristan.

Tristan's head was spinning. Not just from the news, but from his narrow escape. The virus had crippled the flitter carrying him to his death, throwing him clear and killing the thugs Devon had sent. Tristan had escaped with only a few bruises, by some miracle. What Tristan badly needed right now was a week to think this all through and take it in.

But he didn't have a week. He didn't even have minutes. The Doomsday Virus had been released, and it was wreaking havoc on New York. The only person, theoretically, who could stop it was Devon. He had created it to respond only to his commands, enforced by his DNA pattern. The only good thing about this whole mess was that Tristan's DNA was identical to Devon's.

Which meant that Tristan could access anything of Devon's, if he only knew where it was and how to do it. He was the only person in the world who might stand a chance of stopping Devon's murderous plan. It was only a very small chance, but he had to hope that it was enough. Or the human race could be facing the total destruction of the only way of life it knew.

Tristan started running back to his house. Thankfully, the flitter hadn't gone far before it crashed. He was pretty fit, but not up to running a marathon. He couldn't help seeing signs of the destruction all about him as he ran. The streets were, of course, completely free of traffic or pedestrians. Almost nobody had left their homes. Now, nobody *could*. What was going on behind the locked doors, he could only imagine. He doubted that it would be anything nice. Trapped in their homes without power, light, heat, or even fresh air. How long could people last? Days? Hours?

And what if something went wrong? A fire, for example. Or somebody taking sick, maybe with a heart attack. . . .

What about the hospitals? Some might have their own generators, but that wouldn't help much. The medibeds were all computer controlled. Only they knew what dosage of medicine to administer to a sick patient. And some kept people alive on life support — support that would now be cut off. Ambulances wouldn't be able to respond to emergencies — even if people could call them in.

He could still see smoke everywhere from the factories. Devon must have sabotaged their assembly lines to cause trouble before they shut and locked down. There were no aircraft left in the air — those on New York's Net had simply fallen from the sky, as he had witnessed so terribly. At least those on the ground might be safe, even if people were locked aboard.

Unless Devon had made their engines start up and not stop . . . Tristan could picture aircraft plunging off runways into houses, or into other buildings. That would be just the sort of sick twist Devon would have added to the program.

All around, Tristan knew, people were dying — lost, trapped and alone. And this was just the start of how bad things could get if the Net was destroyed.

All business would die. Everything existed now in the Net, for the world's economy was far too complex for anything less than a mainframe to be able to understand. With the mainframes gone, the economy of every country in the world would collapse. No money, no trading, no buying and selling. Not even of food.

And — food itself! To take advantage of the best possible growing conditions, and the best possible prices for their goods, all farms were now automated. A hundred years ago, some farms in North America used computers, but the majority of the world still farmed as if it were a thousand years ago. Now, from America to Africa to Antarctica, humans depended completely upon their machines. There was almost nothing that happened in the world that wasn't in some way touched by computers.

Talk about Armageddon. Civilization would collapse. Millions would die, some immediately, many over the course of months of starvation, thirst, disease, and panic. How could *anyone* want that to happen? Was Devon totally insane? Or just completely without morals? Tristan hadn't talked to him for very long, but his clone seemed to think he was some kind of super-being. Tristan didn't know if this was true — and, if it was, what did that make *him*, since Devon claimed Tristan was his exact clone? Devon certainly had the arrogance to match his claims. But, even granted that, how could anybody want to destroy the human race like this?

And, scariest of all . . . if Tristan *was* Devon's clone (and he only had Devon's word for that; how far could the boy be believed?), then did this mean that the evil arrogance of Devon was somewhere inside Tristan as well?

Was he capable of becoming the criminal that Devon already was?

Tristan didn't want to think that through just yet. He was saved from having to do so by reaching his home. His parents weren't there, and the door to the house had been left open when the thugs had taken Tristan out. That was lucky, all things considered. He wasn't sure there was any power still flowing.

There wasn't. As Tristan had expected, Devon's Doomsday Virus had struck out at the power generator stations quickly. Killing the power increased the chaos and also limited the possibility that anyone could strike back and stop the virus. It was a smart move, one that he himself would have made.

If he were trying to destroy the world. Which he would never ever do, no matter what. Only someone as sick as Devon would even think about it.

Without power, Tristan's Terminal was useless. However, Tristan wasn't beaten yet. He had a spare charged power pack. He rarely needed one, but he always made certain he had it, just in case. His parents, and even Mora, thought he was pretty silly to do this, but events had proven how smart he was, after all. He plugged the pack into his Terminal, and booted it up.

The Screen sprang to life, and he breathed a silent thank-you to the god of computers, whoever he, she, or it was. He couldn't log directly on to the Net — assuming the Net was still there to log on to! — because his account had been wiped out in the first, accidental release of the virus. Instead, he used a backdoor connection and the command sequence to log on to the police computer. He'd stolen the access codes from Inspector Shimoda when she'd called to question him, and he felt no guilt at all logging on to the forbidden computer.

Nothing happened, and Tristan had a twisted feeling in his gut that Devon had indeed destroyed the police computer. Then the Screen flickered to life, and Tristan let some of his fears evaporate. The computer was still up, but working slower than normal. It had to be located somewhere outside of New York City, then, and was still unaffected by the virus.

But for how long?

The computer was working at its maximum capacity, which was why it was so slow. Everybody who could was probably hacked into it, since it was one of the few local servers still operating. Tristan scrambled to get his Terminal to work. It was sluggish, but he finally managed to get into Computer Control.

Tristan breathed a sigh of relief. It was still there, and still functioning. The virus hadn't penetrated it yet. Tristan wondered why. Nobody had known that the Doomsday Virus was being released. What had kept it from wiping out Computer Control?

* * *

New York was like a war zone. It was wonderful. Devon smiled as he watched the images flashing across his Screens. They were too swift for him to catch them all, of course, but he did see many images that amused and pleased him. The Game was being played well, and he was winning, hands down. His genius was creating the wave of chaos that would shortly engulf the whole Earth.

On one Screen: a factory gone rampant. It was some sort of processing place, where metal was refined, purified, and then cast into machines. With the death of the computers, everything instantly stopped. Vats of molten metals stopped in their paths, but inertia meant that the vats swung upward. . . . Red-hot metal cascaded down, melting machines, killing people, and starting fires everywhere. The safety equipment was dead, so the fires caught and spread. Doors and windows were sealed, so the few human workers in the factory couldn't escape the roaring, killing flames.

A second Screen: Kennedy Interplanetary Spaceport. Without computer controls to land, aircraft simply fell from the sky. Their onboard computers, linked to the airport mainframe, also died. Pilots lost control of their crafts. Wings locked, engines fell silent, and the planes could no longer fly. Everything in the air spluttered, stalled, and fell. Houses and roads were wrecked as hundreds of tons of uncontrolled metal slammed into them. More explosions, more fires, more destruction, spreading everywhere.

Another Screen — one of Devon's personal favorites! — showed Times Square. The famous billboard was temporarily immune to the Virus. Instead, he had programmed it to show loops of old monster vids, with Godzilla and other creatures stomping New York to the ground. And, under it, a scroll that read: DIE, SUCKERS, DIE!!!!!

Fun.

On another Screen, Devon watched the Bronx Zoo. He'd programmed all of the cages to automatically open before the system shut down. Animals wandered outside, most of them free for the first time in their lives. Some, naturally, were harmless. They stayed within their environments, happy with where they lived.

Others, however, sensed freedom and food beyond. The great predators — lions, tigers, and wolves — all came out. The few reality visitors panicked and ran screaming. Devon shook his head.

"Not smart," he murmured, watching the enraged

predators chase and catch the fleeing people. “Game over,” he muttered to the victims before switching to another view.

It was all quite wonderful. Thanks to his genius, he was destroying everything that mankind had built up over centuries. The power of ultimate destruction was his, and he had loosed it. The world as it had once been would die, and the new world would begin.

A new world where Devon and Quietus had control. And Devon would wrest control of Quietus from its current leaders. It was simply a matter of time before that happened.

All in all, this was turning out to be a good day, after all. His pesky, moral-filled clone was destroyed, which made him feel a lot better. True, he’d been forced to unleash the Doomsday Virus earlier than he was supposed to, but he’d been given no choice. Somebody had managed to trace him, and if he hadn’t released it early, he might never have been free to do so later on.

For the first time, Devon felt a twinge. Quietus wouldn’t be very happy. His contact with the group, the Malefactor, would be furious. The group had their own plans that they had wanted to mature before the release of the Doomsday Virus. And those plans had been interrupted. The Malefactor would be angry, but surely he would understand that Devon had had no choice in the matter. Devon wasn't sure what the Malefactor could do to punish him, since there had never been a need for punishment before. Devon had always exceeded Quietus's demands on him. But this time . . .

Devon knew that the Malefactor would have a threat to level at Devon. It made sense. Quietus would want to make certain that Devon stayed in line. His stomach knotted as he considered the point. What would they do to him? They couldn't do anything too nasty, because they still needed him very badly. And he had finished off his clone, their backup copy in case Devon needed to be . . . replaced. So they were stuck with having Devon intact and willing to cooperate.

The more he thought about it, the more Devon was certain that Quietus could do nothing much to punish him. Especially since his Doomsday Virus was working perfectly. Wasn't New York City proof of that?

He turned back to watching his Screens again, happy to see the results of his work. The city was dying, and *he* had made this possible.

Nobody else. Just Devon.

And then he was struck by something else. He almost stopped breathing. Then he whipped out his speedboard and started to type in frantic questions and commands.

An icy certainty started to freeze in his mind as he attacked his Terminal. Yes, New York City was dead as it could be . . . but nowhere else was.

Why wasn't the virus spreading? Why wasn't the world crumbling down to dust and decay?

What was happening? Or, rather, what was *not* happening?

Inspector Shimoda's call was finally answered. She wasn't sure whether to be relieved or terrified when she saw the tiny face of her boss, Peter Chen, the head of Net Security. "Sir," she acknowledged. "How bad is it?"

"As bad as it could be." He looked furious and scared at the same time. "Do you know anything about this, Inspector?" he demanded. "Your mission, after all, was to *stop* precisely this from happening! Do you have any reason why I shouldn't fire you this instant?"

Shimoda swallowed. It was bad enough to be yelled at by her boss; it was worse that the girl, Genia, was here, listening to every word and smirking. Genia was a thief, and only working with Shimoda out of necessity. She seemed to be enjoying what she heard.

"Well, there may not be any need for you to fire me," Shimoda replied. "I'm trapped in my apartment, and I'm sure I'm likely to be dead before I can escape."

"I'm inclined to leave you there," Chen growled. "Except that there isn't anyone else I can rely on right now with your level of expertise. I'm sending a rescue crew to get you out, and they'll bring a portable Terminal with them. I don't know how you've managed it, but you seem to have blocked the virus's release worldwide. I want you to keep that going. Chen, out."

The Screen went dead. Genia scowled.

"What did he mean about you having blocked the virus?" she asked. "I don't remember you doing anything like that."

"Nor do I," Shimoda confessed. "But, apparently, *something* is blocking the virus, and Chen thinks it's me."

"Don't tell him otherwise!" Genia snapped, looking scared. "They're coming to rescue us only because they think you're doing something. If they find out you're not, then we may get bumped to the back of the line, and not get rescued until the anniversary of our deaths."

Shimoda felt a twinge of guilt about lying to her boss. It didn't last long under the practical consideration that

Genia had raised. Besides, Shimoda had never said that she'd done anything; it was Chen who had assumed she was up to something.

But since *she* hadn't done anything . . . who had? And what was it that they'd done?

2

Tristan could hardly believe what he had discovered: The virus was, for the moment, contained. It had ravaged through every system in New York City, and some of the outlying areas. Those were as dead as possible, all life leeched from them. But that was all. The virus wasn't spreading further into the Net.

Suddenly, Tristan understood. With a yelp of joy, he realized what had to be happening. His fingers flew over the speedboard, faster than the sluggish backdoor link could keep up with. And he had the answer he was looking for. Who could possibly have designed anything to stop a virus made by one of the most brilliant hackers in the world?

Who but his clone!

In the excitement and stress of all he'd been through, Tristan had forgotten that he'd been on-line when the virus had been released. He had, without really thinking about it, set loose his guard dogs, and told them to breed and stop the virus. He'd done it only to buy himself some time. But it seemed his guard dogs were better than he had ever imagined. They had bred like crazy, taking over programs and functions from any source they could. And they had turned around and attacked the Doomsday Virus.

They were holding it at bay. As fast as the virus destroyed one of the guard dogs, a new one took its place. Even the virus couldn't destroy Tristan's programs with ease. Because, clearly, both programs had been designed by almost identical minds.

Joy surged through Tristan. He felt like yelling and dancing. He'd done it! He'd stopped the virus! And without actually knowing he was doing so.

Then reality sank in, and he collapsed back into his chair.

His guard dogs had stopped the virus. *For now . . .* There was no telling how long they could keep doing so.

They were being destroyed, maybe hundreds of them every second, to keep the virus at bay. The guard dogs were breeding fast enough now, but they were in a sense a little like the virus itself: They bred by taking data and programs from elsewhere and converting them into copies of themselves. Which meant that they were bound to be spotted . . . and once they were found, people might think that *they* were the virus, and try to destroy them.

Which would set the *real* virus free!

How long did he have? Tristan didn't have the vaguest idea. Right now, the police were bound to be dealing only with the main disaster. Computer Control itself would be probing the Net to see what was going on. They employed many of the best programmers in the world, and one of them was bound to find the guard dogs. . . .

Doomsday wasn't beaten. It was just being held at bay. It was as if he were in a mine with the roof collapsing. One beam held it in place, but the beam was straining and breaking. Eventually, it would snap, and everything would collapse.

That was what would happen here. If anyone interfered with the guard dogs, the virus would break free. And this time *nothing* would be able to stop it.

Tristan's palms were sweating. A tornado of fear was

sucking hope out of him, leaving only despair. What could he do? Call Computer Control and tell them what was happening? But why would they believe him? The guard dogs would look like the virus, and he couldn't imagine them believing him if he told them not to touch it. They'd put him on Ice forever.

What could he do? His mind was a complete blank.

When Inspector Shimoda reached Computer Control in Jersey City, she discovered it was a madhouse of activity. She tried to ignore the noise and bustle as people headed in every direction, trying to salvage what they could from the dead city of New York. She tuned out the noise of the emergency vehicles racing toward the locked-in metropolis, to focus on the portable Terminal she'd been given. Genia hovered at her shoulder, trying to see what was happening, and also distracted by everyone rushing around them. Shimoda couldn't blame the young girl. In one respect, at least, this whole business had to be quite exciting.

It was hard to get a picture of what was actually happening in New York. Rescue teams were attempting to get in and extricate people from buildings. Others were working to replace some of the more essential mainframes and get the power back on-line. That was complicated by the fact that the virus was still ravaging the systems. Putting in a new computer would be like throwing meat to starving lions. It wouldn't last long. So connections were being severed with the New York computer grid, and new ones were being created to New Jersey. All of this would take time, of course. And while that was being done, people were dying.

Kennedy Spaceport was a terrible mess. Not only had several planes crashed, so had one Starliner, scattering radioactive fuel over the area, creating yet another new disaster. Kennedy had been completely closed down, and Schwarzenegger Spaceport in Newark was trying to bring in all remaining flights. But they were overloaded, and it was getting bumpy. . . .

None of that was Shimoda's concern right now. There was nothing she could do to help out there. What she had to do was to confirm her suspicions that Tristan was the culprit behind the virus and then arrest him. And, of course, kill the virus. If only it were that simple!

The inspector had her portable Terminal working, and logged on through a New Jersey connection. That way, she could approach the New York Net from a backdoor connection and avoid the virus. Genia was breathing down her neck, her own eyes glued to the Screen as well. Shimoda didn't complain; Genia might be able to offer some good insights.

It took time, but Shimoda isolated several strands that she required. There were mechanisms holding the virus in, preventing it from spreading. After a few moments, she realized that she'd seen these things before. When she had first tried tracking down the criminal, before she had realized it was Tristan Connor, these guard dogs had held off her search engine for quite a few minutes. These were identical hounds, and had to be part of the criminal's plan. But why release the virus and then contain it?

Unless . . .

Shimoda's skin went cold. The villain had deliberately targeted New York as an example of what he could do. The guard dogs were holding the virus at bay — for now. The criminal was probably intending to ask for blackmail. If he didn't get what he wanted, he'd call off the guard dogs and let the virus ravage everything. It was a coldblooded attempt to extort money from the world by holding the threat of destruction over its head. . . .

She *had* to stop it! But how? She could hardly create something like the guard dogs quickly enough to help out here — if at all. They were very sophisticated programs. She looked up at Genia, sudden hope dawning.

"You're the self-proclaimed computer genius," Shimoda said. "Can you create something to devour the virus?"

For once, Genia looked unsure of herself. Her cockiness seemed deflated. "I don't know," she confessed. "A day ago I'd have been certain I could outwrite anybody's programs. But those guard dogs and that virus are nasty pieces of work. Whoever did them is absolutely brilliant. I can tell the workmanship of any program, and they're definitely the work of one mind. And I've seen it somewhere before —"

"Where?" Shimoda asked urgently. Now that Genia mentioned it, Shimoda could see a sort of family resemblance in the two programs. "Wait," she added, her mind in overdrive. "I think I know." She pulled up some of the school records — thankfully centralized out on Long Island and not part of New York Net! — and studied one of the geographic problem programs.

"Identical workmanship," Genia said within seconds. "That's your guy."

Shimoda nodded in satisfaction. "Tristan Connor. Just as I suspected." She looked up from her Terminal, and located the emergency dispatcher. "I've found our criminal," she informed him. "And I need to get out a Shield Priority Alert for the arrest of one Tristan Connor." She glanced at Genia. "If we get him fast enough, maybe we can force him to shut down the virus."

"And if we can't?" asked Genia. She looked pleased at being part of the team.

"Then let's hope you really are the genius you claim to be." Shimoda sighed. "That virus is way out of my league; let's hope it's still within yours."

That wiped the smile off the girl's face. But she settled down at the Terminal to study what they could see of the guard dogs. Shimoda didn't have much confidence in their ability to solve the problem. But, unless they captured Tristan Connor, it was the only hope the world had.

Doomsday was getting closer by the second.

Tristan was in a haze of depression. His whole world was collapsing, and he badly needed help. His parents had already proven they were of no use to him. He didn't exactly blame them for what they had done. They had lied, after all, thinking that they were protecting him. They had been warned by a mysterious Dr. Taru that Tristan must never know he was adopted, or a group called Quietus would aim to kill the boy. And, as it had turned out, the doctor had been telling the truth. The problem was that his parents had still lied to him for years by claiming him as their son, even if for the best of reasons. Right now, Tristan couldn't bring himself to trust them again.

Besides which, he wasn't exactly sure where they were. All he knew was that they weren't at home.

No, he had to have someone he could talk to, someone he could trust. Someone who'd be there for him, no matter what. In other words, his girlfriend, Mora Worth. Mora understood and sympathized with him, and she'd help him. Maybe she could think of somewhere to hide out. The police were bound to search her house sooner or later.

Maybe they were even there now. Tristan didn't think it was possible, but Inspector Shimoda had seemed efficient and determined. It was hard to judge what she might have done. But Tristan had to take that chance — he needed help very badly right now, and he couldn't stay here.

What if he gave himself up, and explained everything? Maybe the police would believe him? Maybe they'd help?

"Yeah, right," he muttered to himself, as he gathered a few belongings into his pack. He could just see it now, when he tried to explain that *he* wasn't guilty, it was his evil twin. . . . A plot right off a soap vid! Besides, everybody knew that cloning people was illegal, and had been for almost a hundred years. The shields would think his story was the feeblest excuse that they had ever heard. Unless he could actually tell them where Devon was; then they could capture him and prove Tristan's story.

So he couldn't let the shields get to him until he'd tracked down Devon, and could prove he wasn't lying. Besides which, the only way to stop the virus was at its source. If he could find the Terminal it was being generated from and close down the link, then he could examine the virus at rest and work out a way to destroy it. If Devon could create it, Tristan was certain he could destroy it. With time.

Which was something he probably didn't have a whole lot of.

Tristan had decided on his course of action, but he was far from happy with his decision. It was, at best, a slim chance. And while he was trying to track down Devon, the other youth was hardly likely to just sit still. Right now he probably thought that Tristan was dead. But when his thugs didn't report in, Devon was bound to wonder. And when he discovered the truth, Devon would certainly try to kill Tristan again.

Another reason for Tristan to track down Devon first. If he could . . .

Slinging the pack over his shoulder, Tristan left

his house again. He only hoped he had what he would need in there — and that Mora would come through with everything else. He felt warm just thinking about her. It would be nice to see her again, despite the trouble he was in. It seemed like forever since he'd last been with her, though at most it could only be a few hours. But so much had happened in that short span of time. His whole life and his whole world had changed.

The smoke from the direction of New York City reminded him that it was not only his own life that had changed. The smoke from the dying metropolis was just a promise of much worse things to come if Devon were not found and defeated.

Tristan couldn't give up now.

Barker stood in the Underworld, looking up, amazed.

He'd been down here, below New York City, for over twenty years. Like most of the inhabitants of the Underworld, he'd once had a place in real society. Then that society decided it didn't need him, and had thrown him away, like human trash. He'd ended up in the old, decaying city beneath the modern city. Here the dregs of the human race tried to live. Many didn't make it, but Barker had. He was smart, he was strong, and he was now without many traces of morality. Surviving in the

Underworld tended to burn out most of what polite society considered necessary.

Living below New York City, there was always a reminder of your place in the world. Several stories above the base of the city was the new "ground level," where the powers-that-be had simply laid a new floor and used that to build upon. Anything below it was left to rot and decay. Everything above was fresh and bright.

Until now.

The lights of New York had always shone down into the permanent gloom of the Underworld. There were no streetlights down here; most of the faint illumination had bled through from above. But, suddenly, that glow had died out.

So had most of the perpetual noise from above. The machineries of mankind had fallen silent. The flitters had stopped. Even the air-conditioning had quieted. There was a sound like a large intake of breath, and then absolute silence from the world above.

Barker didn't know what this meant, exactly. It was something he'd never experienced before, and something he'd never expected to happen. Hurriedly, he gestured to the members of his gang. They gathered around, dropping whatever had interested them before. "Listen," Barker commanded, and they obediently listened.

"I don't hear nothing," one man muttered.

"That's the point," Barker said, his excitement rising. "Nor do I. No power being used at all. It's like the city is dead. And you know what that means?" His men looked at him blankly. They were loyal to him, but not exactly bright. He often wished there was just one of them with whom he could have a reasonable conversation. He might as well have wished to be crowned king of the world. Patiently, he explained, "No power means no alarms. It means no shields. It means nobody can get out of their homes. It means," he concluded, "that we can go on a binge, stealing whatever we find. And nobody can stop us. Boys, this is our lucky day!"

Finally understanding what he meant, his gang swarmed after Barker, upward into the world above.

This was going to be the best day of their lives.

Tristan made it to the Worth house, panting from the unusual exertion. He exercised at home usually, a half-hour a day in his Virtual Gym to stay in shape. But all of the running around he'd done today was more than he was used to, and he felt exhausted. He wished he could take a break and do something mindless, like surfing the Net. But there was no time for that.

The Worth house still had power, he could see, even though they were slightly closer to the city. They were still outside the area hit by the virus. For that, Tristan was thankful. This meant that their Terminals were likely to be still on-line, and if he used one of those he could start his search. Then he'd have to leave and find somewhere else to hide before the shields could trace him.

He tapped his code on the entry pad, and the house-comp signaled whoever was home that he was at the door. A moment later, Mora opened it. She looked pale and tired, which was hardly surprising.

"Tristan!" she exclaimed. "What are you doing here?"

"I need help," he answered, brushing past her and into the house. "The shields are probably after me. They have to think I've set some virus loose in the city by now."

"What are you talking about?" she asked. "What have you done?"

"I haven't done *anything*," he protested. "But I'm sure that they'll think I have." He dropped his pack beside the door. "Look, I'll explain everything as I go along, but it's vital that I get to use one of your Terminals now." He looked around the hallway. "Can I use the one in your room?"

Mora looked confused and troubled. "I suppose so," she said. "But you're in trouble, you know."

"Tell me about it." He hurried to her room. Her Terminal was beside her bed, and he sat on the bed to switch it on. "It's been a horrible day." Then he blinked. "It's not powering up."

Mora looked at him, her face twisted. "I disconnected it, Tristan," she confessed.

Tristan didn't understand. "What? Why?"

"I'm sorry, Tristan." Mora tapped a code into the wall panel, and the door slid shut.

She was on the outside.

He was trapped on the inside.

He dived for the door, but was too late. Furious, confused, he slammed his hands against the door. It didn't give, of course. "Mora! What are you doing?"

"The shields called us," she said through the door. It sounded as if she were crying. "They told us that you'd released a virus that wiped out all the computers in New York. That you'd caused the deaths of thousands of people. Destruction of property . . . " Her voice trailed off.

"They're wrong, Mora," Tristan said desperately. "They believe that I did that. But I didn't! You know me. You know I'd never do anything like that!"

"Normally, no," she agreed. "But you're not behaving normally. You haven't since you took that fall off our roof, saving Marka's pony. You've been obsessed and intense. Paranoid, even. I think you must have damaged your brain, Tristan. The shields promised that they'd have you tested. It's the best thing. Honestly it is."

"Mora, no!" he screamed. "You don't understand! There's nothing wrong with me! It's my clone — he's the one who did this."

Mora choked back a sob. "Tristan, *listen* to yourself. You don't *have* a clone. Clones are illegal. The shields are right — you have gone mad."

Tristan howled in frustration. "No, don't do this! Let me out of here! I can't be arrested. There's too much to do!"

But there was no reply from the other side of the door. Mora had fled, probably to call the police and tell them that she had Tristan trapped. He hammered on the door again, yelling wordlessly, furious and scared.

Mora — Mora, of all people! — had betrayed him. She believed he was sick and needed help. She believed all the terrible things that the shields had said about him. Tristan collapsed onto the floor, his back against the door. He had thought she loved him, but she neither believed nor trusted him. She had locked him up and sold him out.

His heart felt dead. If the shields took him away, then there was nobody who could stop the virus. Mora could be signing a death warrant for the whole world.

And there was nothing he could do about it. . . .

3

Devon was still enjoying the sights of destruction. He was particularly pleased with the burning skyscrapers, like immense torches in the sky. Flames howled upward, as out-of-town fire flyers attempted to douse the flames. They might as well have tried spitting on the flames for all the good it did. New York City was burning down, and there was very little anyone could do to prevent the spread of the blaze. Most rescue operations centered on getting people out of nearby buildings. But without power, this was a room-by-room evacuation, taking a lot longer than was safe or effective.

Suddenly, all of Devon's Screens went dead. Devon was startled, jerking upright in his chair.

"HOW DARE YOU!"

Devon whipped around to see the image of the Malefactor staring at him. Devon had never seen his image before, only the words of fire he usually wrote in the air. But he had no doubt who this image belonged to. It stood about eight feet tall — obviously enhanced, to disguise his true nature — with a masklike face that was dark and scowling. Devon swallowed, but tried to act as if nothing could possibly be wrong. "Hi."

"You released the Doomsday Virus again!" the Malefactor intoned gravely. "After you were *expressly* forbidden to do so until I gave you permission!"

"True," agreed Devon cautiously. "But not the complete picture. It was a spur-of-the-moment decision, and I simply didn't have the time to call you up and chat about it."

The Malefactor loomed forward. "Your arrogance is very unfortunate," he said ominously. "You are not indispensable to Quietus, you know."

"I wouldn't be so certain about that," Devon answered, hardly bothering to hide his smugness. "I found out all about your clone of me, you know."

"You did *what*?" For the first time, there was confusion and not anger in the voice.

"The clone you had made and hidden," Devon replied. He knew he was inching his way back to being in command here again, whatever the Malefactor thought. "And I think that by now he has ceased to exist. Along with all traces of his DNA. You can't replace me with him now. I'm all you have got to work with. I *am* indispensable." He crossed his arms and smiled at the Malefactor.

The dark figure scowled again. "I don't know how you managed to find out about your clone brother," he said dangerously. "But if you *have* disposed of him, we still don't need *you*. Just some of your DNA. And we could get that from your blood. . . . We don't need the rest of you."

Devon wondered for a second if he had indeed gone too far. "There's no need to get nasty," he said hastily, throwing up his hands. "I'm not a problem to you. Like I said, I didn't have any choice but to release the virus. The shields were tracking it down. If they'd found it, they might have been able to neutralize it. It was time to use it or lose it."

The Malefactor stared at him coldly. "That is not a very good defense," he decided. "The shield is one Inspector Shimoda, and she is being closely monitored by one of our agents. She will not be able to stop us. On the contrary, we can stop her at any time. It is important to us right now that things look like they are being handled. Your stupidity has twice jeopardized our objectives. We are not yet ready for our plan to be set into motion. Yet we are so close. . . . If you have destroyed our chances, rest assured that *we* shall destroy *you*."

The image vanished.

Devon stared at the empty space, and then jumped as all of his Screens came back to life. No doubt about it, he realized — the Malefactor wasn't happy. Perhaps Devon *had* overestimated his own importance in the scheme of things. Perhaps the Malefactor meant to kill him.

In which case, there was no need for Devon to be here to run his plans. He could go anywhere and have access to all that he needed. There was no need for him to be physically present.

And it might be a good idea to disappear from the Malefactor's view for a while. . . .

The man who called himself the Malefactor turned from his projection equipment, seething. The boy was getting far too full of himself, and was absolutely infuriating. It had once seemed to be a great idea to raise Devon without outside contact, to be the greatest computer genius the world had ever known. And it seemed to have worked, at least as far as his computer skills went. The boy still had no concept of his true place in the scheme of things.

But how had he found out about the clone? And had he *really* somehow managed to destroy him? If he had, it meant that the hold Quietus had over Devon had loosened. The thought was sickening. Devon *had* to be firmly controlled, until he was of no further use to them.

Only then could he be destroyed.

The Malefactor pressed his hands to his aching temples, rubbing gently in circles. Devon's first premature release of the virus had alerted Computer Control to the existence of Quietus, which was terrible. His *second* release of the virus was causing even more chaos. The Malefactor's plans were not in place to take full advantage of the virus yet. It was impossible to advance them too far or too fast. But he would have to try.

It would involve two calls. The first was the trickiest. Powering up his imaging device, the Malefactor sent the false picture of himself to the receiving Terminal. There was a delay of several minutes; the Malefactor hated the time lag involved in sending messages to other planets. Finally, though, his Screens lit up with the view of Ares One, seated at his desk. Behind the man, through the window, lay the red plains of Mars.

"Malefactor," Ares One replied, looking worried. "I didn't expect to be contacted yet."

"I know you didn't," the Malefactor replied. "I would not have done so, except something slightly amiss has occurred. The Doomsday Virus was released too early. We must bring forward the target date. How soon can you be ready?" He paused, knowing that it would take several minutes for the reply to come back. As he waited, he noticed a small light flashing on his panel; someone was calling him. . . . He blanked out the camera, so that Ares One wouldn't see or hear whatever was said, and clicked on the new call.

It was the Controller, looking worried. "Malefactor," he said, his voice tense, "the situation is getting desperate."

"I'm not interested in your problems," the Malefactor snarled. "I don't care if every person in the city dies. Deal with it." He moved to cut off the call.

"That isn't it!" the Controller exclaimed. "The virus has been stopped."

"What?" This was surely impossible — if Devon was to be believed. "How can that be?"

"We don't know." The Controller was understandably tense and agitated. "Shimoda is tracking it, but it seems confined to New York at the moment. Not only that, but —" he swallowed — "Devon's clone seems to be involved. She has identified him as Tristan Connor, and ordered his arrest."

"What?" How could matters get any worse? "The clone has turned up *here*?" No wonder Devon had discovered his existence. . . . Everything seemed to be falling apart. "She must not be allowed to gain access to this . . . Connor. If we cannot capture him first, then have him eliminated. Make certain that Shimoda's trail goes cold."

"Wouldn't it be simpler to dispose of Shimoda herself?" asked the Controller.

"Simpler, yes," agreed the Malefactor. "But stupider. If she dies, then she'll be replaced. Perhaps with somebody even more efficient. She has made a number of mistakes so far, and I like that in her. She's more controllable than her replacement might be. Besides, there's no way to kill her now without it being obvious why it was done. No, let her follow all the leads she likes. Just make certain that your men reach this Connor child first. Abduct or murder him, but don't let Shimoda get to him. And *make sure* she does not learn he's a clone." He switched off the channel, and was in time for Ares One to answer.

"We are working at speeding up the schedule, as you

requested. As soon as I have an estimated time when we can strike, I will contact you. Quietus shall succeed; I pledge my life to that."

You do indeed, the Malefactor thought. Aloud, he said, "Good. My best wishes to your family. I trust that they are all well. Continue the excellent work." He ceased his own transmission, and sat back to think.

All that he and Quietus had worked for was so close to fruition. And now, after so many years, everything seemed to be going wrong. The appearance of the clone, far too soon. The release of the virus before it was time. The trapping of it in the New York Net. But this reversal would not last long. He would regain control of the situation shortly.

It was definitely time to take steps with Devon. If the clone was dead, then Shimoda was not a problem. If the clone was alive, however, she could not be allowed to use him. The clone hadn't been raised as Devon had; he had been placed within a normal family and allowed to grow, unaware of the truth. So — what had gone wrong?

"Thank you for your concern. We are all quite fine."

The Malefactor looked up, startled. It was just Ares One, answering his last message, of course. Now he was gone, too, leaving the Malefactor alone to brood.

There were problems, but they could all be dealt with. Soon.

Genia was almost enjoying herself. She'd been a loner for most of her life. Her mother had died when Genia was young, and her father had been sent to prison long before that. Left to fend for herself in the Underworld, Genia had made a life there. Quite a nice one, too, thanks to her hacking skills. She had stolen money from those who could afford it (and some probably never even missed it) and used it to finance herself. Everything had been fine until she'd managed to capture a fragment of the Doomsday Virus.

Then its inventor, apparently this Tristan Connor, had tried to kill her. She'd been forced to cut a deal for protection with the shields. Now she was on the inside looking out, for once. Inspector Shimoda wasn't a bad sort, and Genia could almost like the young woman. She was only a competent programmer, but she was a nice enough person, and she was taking care of Genia, as she'd promised.

Genia wolfed down more of her lunch, watching what the inspector was doing on her Screen. The woman had managed to get fairly close to the guard dogs, and was trying to figure them out. "I'd be real careful," Genia advised her, between bites of shrimp mei fun. She pointed at the code lines with her chopsticks. "Those guard dogs are the only things holding that virus at bay. You mess them up, and the virus is going to get a lot more than just New York City."

"Don't you think I know that?" asked Shimoda, her face strained. "But I have to try and understand them if I'm to duplicate them. Right now, if Connor decides to cancel them, there's nothing to prevent the virus from spreading. We have to have some way to keep the virus harnessed. Until we can destroy it."

"Makes sense," Genia agreed. "But I don't think you'll ever manage that. No offense, but you're not good enough to write a program like those dogs."

"I'm starting to suspect you're right," the inspector admitted.

"I know I'm right." Genia finished the last of the food, and tossed the package and chopsticks at the recycler. She missed, but didn't let that bother her. "Let me have a Terminal, and I'll be able to manage it for you. I'm a lot better at this than you are."

Shimoda was tempted, that was clear. But Genia could also see that the policewoman was worried, which was understandable, given Genia's criminal background.

"Look," Genia said, "I steal stuff over the Net. If the virus kills the Net, I'm out of a living. It's in my best interest to help you. Besides, that Connor kid tried to have me killed, and I want to pay him back for that."

After a moment, Shimoda nodded. She tapped at her wrist-comp. "I've put in for a second machine for you," she explained. "When it comes, get busy. And . . . thanks."

Genia grinned. It felt nice being on the side of law and order for a change. But she hoped she wouldn't get to like the feeling too much. She realized that as soon as this crisis was over, she'd be thanked and then kicked out again to fend for herself.

Except, she was dead wrong about that.

The man called Peter Chen came into the crowded, noisy office, and glared at the inspector. Genia remembered that he was Shimoda's boss. He looked really unhappy about something.

"What do you think you're doing?" he snapped.

Shimoda looked up, a faint frown on her face. "Trying to work out a barrier to keep the virus contained in case the guard dogs are recalled."

"I don't mean *that*," Chen replied. "That's fine." He suddenly jerked a finger at Genia. "I mean *that*."

The inspector cocked her head to one side, puzzled.

"Genia is helping me. She's very skilled with computers, and I think that, with her help —"

"She's a thief!" Chen exploded. "She doesn't have an Implant-Chip! She's from the Underworld. She shouldn't be helping you, she should be locked up!"

Genia was stunned, but Shimoda rose to her feet, anger on her face and in her voice. "She has helped me out already," she snapped back. "And she came to me for police protection. Connor tried to have her killed. She needs looking after."

"That's not your place to decide!" Chen spat back. "I'm in charge of this department, and I make decisions like that. We can't go around offering police protection to every thief and cheat from the Underworld!"

"I gave her my word," Shimoda said simply.

"It's not your decision," her boss replied angrily. "You've broken department rules once too often, Shimoda!" He turned to two policewomen working nearby. "You, both of you! Take this piece of human trash down to processing! She's a thief, and is to be tried as such. Now!"

Genia turned, looking for a way out. But it was no use. The room was too crowded for her to run. Besides, she was inside shield headquarters. Even if she got out of the room, the place was crawling with police. Escape was impossible. As the two woman grabbed hold of her arms, Genia looked at Shimoda in disgust and disappointment. "You gave me your word you'd look after me," she said. "So this is what it's worth?"

"You'll be well looked after," Chen assured her, a faint smile on his face at last. "Nobody will harm you once you're in jail for the rest of your miserable life."

"You are dishonoring me," Shimoda said, in a deadly quiet voice. "You should not do this thing."

"Enough!" barked Chen. "You should never have tried to make a bargain with a crook in the first place. This is being noted in your file, and an official reprimand will be issued. If you want to keep your job, then continue with locating and destroying the virus. Put this foolish girl from your mind." He leaned over the inspector. "Do you understand me?"

After a moment, Shimoda nodded. She gave Genia a guilt-ridden glance, and then sat back down at her Terminal. Genia almost felt sorry for the woman. Almost.

Mostly, she was furious.

Chen turned to the policewomen. "I told you to take her to processing!" he snapped. "Do it now, and make sure she's in a cell. Search her first. She's very resourceful. I don't want a jail break."

The women nodded, and forced Genia to start walking. Seething, but helpless, she obeyed. Once again, she had been betrayed by the official world. She should have known better than to think she could trust these people to be kind to her. What a jerk she had been! And now she would pay for it.

Jailed . . . for the rest of her life.

4

Tristan was too depressed to even think about escaping Mora's room. Mora — his Mora! — didn't believe him. She had accepted that he was a crook and a murderer. She had trapped him and then called the shields. Everything would collapse now.

Tristan sat with his back to the door, feeling desperately empty and alone. There was nothing to motivate him any longer. He had been let down by everyone he had ever believed in or trusted. His parents had lied to him about his true identity; his girlfriend had disbelieved him and sold him out to the police; and his enemy was closer to him than any of them — a person who shared everything with Tristan, down to the last cell in his body — and yet was also so alien. Devon possessed the same potential and skills as Tristan, and yet he was a self-absorbed, amoral creep who had willingly killed thousands of people without it bothering him . . . and who might yet kill millions more. His actions would make the Asiatic Flu Death of 2023 look mild by comparison. That had only killed a third of the world's population. Devon might kill more than half.

And just how different was Devon from Tristan, after all? They shared so much — did they share the same potential for evil? Was Tristan fooling himself when he believed he was better than his clone?

Did any of it matter any longer? The police believed that Tristan was the guilty party. He could hardly blame them, given the evidence against him. Eventually, they might realize that they had the wrong person, but by that time Devon would probably be unstoppable. Tristan wished Mora was into electronics or something, so there was a chance of finding something useful here, something he might be able to utilize to escape with. But she liked clothes and jewelry and things like that. Her closets were filled with nothing else. Not a hyperdriver, nor a stack-card in the place, unless he tore her disconnected Terminal apart. And he didn't even have an old-fashioned screwdriver to do that with!

It was frustrating, scary, and depressing, all at the same time. To be trapped like this, unable to do anything at all —

He almost fell over backward when the door abruptly slid open. Catching himself in time, he started to stand. The shields had arrived faster than he had expected. And then he blinked, confused.

It wasn't the police; it was Mora's kid sister, Marka. The eight-year-old gave him a thin smile and signaled for him to be quiet. Then she gestured for him to follow her. Quietly, puzzled, Tristan did so. He heard Mora on the phone in the living room, and they hurried past swiftly and silently. In the hallway, he scooped up his pack and slung it over his shoulder. Then Marka opened the door. Together they hurried outside.

"What are you doing?" Tristan asked her softly. He didn't want them to be heard by Mora.

"Setting you free," Marka said, with the solemn determination of her age. "Mora's such a jerk, believing what the police said about you." She sniffed. "*I* didn't, not for a second. You'd never do what they said."

"No," Tristan said, feeling remarkably happy. Someone believed in him! "I never would."

"I knew that." Marka grinned. "You saved my pony," she added. "I owed you one." Then she threw her arms about his neck and kissed his cheek. "Besides, I always thought Mora didn't deserve you. You should have waited till I grew up."

"I'm beginning to think I should," Tristan agreed, laughing softly. "But I've got to go now. I'm the only one who might be able to stop the real villain. I can't let the police arrest me." He kissed Marka's cheek in return. "I won't ever forget what you've done for me."

"You'd better not," Marka answered. "I think we're engaged."

Tristan laughed again, as he waved and ran off. Keeping to the shrubbery as much as possible, he started running back toward his own house. The police wouldn't look there yet, and maybe he could find inspiration while he ran. Though he was tremendously uplifted by Marka's childish faith in him, he needed more than that to get to work. He needed, first of all, a Terminal. And then he needed to be able to disguise his on-line self so that the police couldn't track him that way.

And he didn't have even the vaguest idea how to do that. . . .

Mora felt sick at what she had done. She had let Tristan down, she knew. She'd seen the accusation in his eyes. But what other choice did she have? The police had absolute proof that he was the person who'd created the virus. When it had wiped out the bank where Tristan's father was a vice president, she'd believed his story that it had been an accident. But now the virus had almost destroyed New York! She'd seen the pictures from the Newsbots still flying, and was sickened. Burned-out buildings, with smoking bodies being carried out. Crashed flitters, with more corpses. Factories that had exploded, aircraft that had fallen from the sky. Thousands and thousands of people were still trapped in the city. Some would not survive. Buildings were aflame and collapsing. There had been no disaster like this since the Middle Ages, when wandering armies had ransacked and burned whole towns.

And, throughout the whole thing, Tristan's guilt.

How could he have done such a thing? The only explanation she had was his accident. He'd hurt his head, and on vid dramas that often led people to do strange, mad things. That must be what had happened to Tristan. He'd never have done this otherwise. But ever since he'd come home from the hospital, he'd been behaving very oddly and secretively. He needed help, and she had to make sure he got it. He had to hate her right now, but when he was better he'd understand and forgive her.

Tears trickled down her cheeks as she thought about what she had done, and how Tristan must loathe her. But it was the right course of action.

"Huh?" The policewoman on the phone Screen had spoken, but Mora had missed it.

"The arresting squad will be there in ten minutes," the woman repeated. "You are not in any immediate danger from the fugitive?"

"Danger?" From *Tristan*? Even if he was sick, he'd never hurt her! "No, he's locked up and can't get out. He'll be safe there till your men arrive." She switched off the phone.

There was the chime of someone at the door. Who could that be? Visitors rarely came here. Mora walked briskly to the door; her parents were home, but both were at work in their separate rooms, and probably hadn't heard the chimes. Marka was at school in her own room, and she never answered the door, anyway.

Five men were there, all armed with stasers. The lead one flashed an official chip at her. "Police," he snapped. "Where's the criminal?"

"Police?" Mora frowned. "The lady said you'd be another ten minutes."

"Traffic was light," the shield answered. "We made good time. The criminal?"

"Oh." Mora shook her head. "In my room. It's this way." She led them down the hallway, noticing that they had their guns ready to use. Two of them moved off into the house, probably to block exits, or something. No doubt it was their standard procedure. Reaching her room, she hesitated with her hand over the entry pad.

"We're ready," the shield said, his face grim and set, mistaking her hesitation for fear.

She was just worried about Tristan. "You're not going to shoot him?" she asked.

The man shook his head. "We need him alive," he answered. "He's got to tell us how to halt this virus. These guns are set to stun."

"Oh." Relieved, she reached out and touched the pad, keying in her code. The door slid open.

There was no sign of Tristan. The lead two shields moved into her room, the third one staying behind to cover her, probably in case Tristan made a break for it. It was really reassuring, the way that they were protecting her.

The first shield came out a moment later, his face scowling. "He's not in there."

"What?" Mora couldn't understand. She looked past him, as if she might be able to find Tristan where they had not. "But . . . but I locked him in!" she exclaimed. "He *must* be in there."

"He isn't," the shield said flatly. He turned to her keypad by the door and scanned it quickly. "When did you lock him in?"

"About fifteen minutes ago," she answered. What was going on here?

"Somebody opened the door about ten minutes ago," the policeman said. "From the outside." He turned to one of the other shields. "Bring in everyone in the house. Someone has been aiding a fugitive." He glared harshly at Mora. "Possibly you." He gestured with his gun. "Move into the main room."

"But . . . why would I let him out?" Mora protested. "He needs help; he's done some terrible things."

"You're his girlfriend," the man answered. "Maybe you called the police to set up an alibi for yourself, and then helped him. It doesn't matter." He tapped her lightly with the barrel of the staser. "Now move, or I'll drag you."

Mora could see that he was perfectly serious, so she walked swiftly into the family room. The other shields, who had moved out through the house, were there — along with her parents and Marka. Her father was fuming.

"What do you people think you're doing?" he exclaimed. "I'm a very important person at Jacoby and Stern. These . . . these *thugs* of yours disconnected me while I was in the middle of a very important financial transaction."

"My heart bleeds for you," the head shield grunted. "You're all under arrest."

"What?" Her father's yelp was echoed by the whole family. They all started to protest, until the shield held up his staser warningly.

"One or more of you let a wanted felon escape. *Helped* him escape. Until we determine who, you're all under suspicion. And that means I have the authority to arrest every one of you."

Marka stepped forward, her face defiant. "I did it. You can let the rest of them go."

"You?" The shield laughed, something Mora would have said was impossible. "You're a good kid, trying to take the rap. But it won't work." Then his eyes narrowed, and he glared at Mora and her parents. "Unless you're thinking that because she's underage, she can confess and be let off. If so, it won't work." He turned to his men. "Throw them all in the flitter, take them to Computer Central, and then book them."

Mora started forward in shock. "No!" she protested.

"We're law-abiding citizens! I called you when Tristan came here, and caught him for you. You can't arrest us."

"Girl, I just did." The shield ignored her. One of the others grabbed her by the shoulder, not gently.

"Come with me," he growled. "It'll be easier for you." Mora, realizing that she had no option — she could hardly fight off this man-mountain — went along quietly. There was a shield flitter waiting outside the house, with another policeman in it. As they approached it, another shield flitter drew up, and three people jumped out.

The leader hesitated, scowling. "What's going on here?" he asked. "Have you caught the fugitive?"

"No," Mora's escort answered. "The captain's still inside, but we've taken over this site. There's nothing for you here."

"We'll see about that." The policeman hurried inside.

"What's going on?" Mora asked. "Why are there two sets of you?"

"We're a special force," the man holding her answered. "They're just the regulars. They should have been pulled off when we were assigned. Typical bureaucratic mess-up." He gestured with his pistol. "Into the flitter, kid. You're going into the judicial system right now."

Mora hung her head, ashamed. She was only glad

that nobody she knew was witnessing this. Being arrested, as if she were a criminal! And all because she did her civic duty, and tried to help her boyfriend get the help he needed.

What would happen to her now?

5

Tristan was in terrible shape. He was physically quite exhausted, but it was his mental state that was the real problem. He had faced too many shocks, one after another, and Mora's betrayal had simply been the final straw. He'd run as far as he could away from the Worth house, and then simply collapsed in someone's garden, cowering behind a bush, in case any shields happened by. There was probably not much point in trying to hide — after all, the Implant Chip in his wrist was a dead giveaway. The police only had to scan as they passed, and they'd pick up the signal from the IC. But, right now, he didn't much care. He just slumped, and gave in to his overwhelming depression.

The whole world had crashed down about him — figuratively and literally. He'd done nothing to deserve any of this. He'd always tried to be kind, and thoughtful, and easygoing. And now look at him — battered and aching, without real parents, and with a clone who wanted him dead. The police were hunting him to throw him in jail for the rest of his life, his girlfriend wanted him in a mental hospital, his clone wanted him in a grave — or, rather, vaporized, so no traces of his DNA existed anywhere.

It was just too much. Tristan couldn't take any more. He wanted to strike out in anger, but he had no target. Not Mora, no matter what she had done to him. He still had feelings for her, even though her turning on him was burning some of them away. He'd like to punch the daylights out of Devon, but he didn't even have a clue where the boy was. He could be anywhere in the world, after all. Tristan had only seen him on a Screen.

The anger inside him began to grow. He'd done his best, and here he was, betrayed, hunted, and despised. Gradually his lethargy was replaced by fury. Why should this have happened to him? Why shouldn't he do something about it? By the time he'd resolved to get moving and fight back, he had gained his second wind. And also some more scary thoughts.

He returned to the site of the flitter crash he had survived. With all of the real problems in New York City, it was unlikely that the authorities had bothered yet with cleaning up the mess, even if there were bodies involved. Because of computer security, accidents were normally high-priority cleanups. All DNA traces had to be removed or burned away, to prevent the unscrupulous from stealing the material and gaining illegal access to the Net.

What Tristan most needed now was access to the Net. And he couldn't do it as himself. . . . If he tried to log on, the shields would track him down through his codes. Every alarm still working in the city would go off if Tristan Connor logged on. Or even if he entered a public building. The IC in his wrist would be scanned by the doorway as he walked through it. The shields would have his Ident-Code in the system by now, and any such scan would again set off all of the alarms.

He had to prevent the police from scanning him. And he couldn't stop them if he had a functioning IC in his wrist. Which meant that he had to get rid of it.

Actually removing it was impossible. Aside from the fact that he'd have to undergo surgery to take the chip out — and he didn't have any anesthetics! — the chip was designed so that if anyone other than an authorized surgeon tried to remove it, there was a fail-safe mechanism in it that ensured the person would bleed to death.

So, that was out. But there was another option.

His hunch had been correct. Nobody had come to the crash site yet. The flitter had stopped burning, and was no more than a framework shell now. He hoped that some of the mechanisms had survived the crash. Smoke still filled the area from where the aircraft he'd seen had impacted. There might be rescue workers there, but they'd hardly pay any attention to him at this flitter. They had more important things on their minds. And everyone else was trapped inside the homes, of course.

The metal was still warm, but not so hot as to burn him if he was quick. Using a snapped-off beam, he pried open the drive mechanism of the flit. He breathed a sigh of relief; a few connectors had melted, but on the whole the engine was intact.

What he needed was the battery. The flits picked up broadcast power to actually move — which was why they crashed when the power cut off — but they had a battery backup that was supposed to power the vehicle to a stop in case of any power outage. It hadn't made any difference in this case, of course, since the flitter's onboard computers had fried along with the main one when the virus was freed, and the command to stop the vehicle had never been sent. So the battery should still be fully charged. . . .

He checked it with the monitor he'd brought along with him in his backpack. Perfect! Now came the really hard part. He had to steel himself to do this, but there was no other way around. The only way to stop his IC from betraying him was to kill it. This meant an applied surge of electricity across its contacts. Shorting the battery through the IC would almost melt it. But not damage him.

He hoped.

Of course, the only way to get that surge through to the IC was painful. He took two wires out of the engine, and prepped the ends. He needed the shielding on them, otherwise the battery would simply discharge through his flesh. And that would be very nasty indeed. The monitor showed him exactly where in his wrist the IC was implanted, and he psyched himself up for the next stage.

Then he plunged the first wire into his wrist, stabbing down at the right spot.

He wanted to scream at the pain burning through his arm, but he didn't dare. That might draw attention to him, and he couldn't afford that. Instead, he clamped his jaws shut, jammed his eyes closed, and tried to ignore the horrible pain.

It didn't work, but after a moment he was able to endure it. His wrist throbbed and burned, but he had to carry on. Ignoring the blood and pain, he used the monitor to check his progress. Naturally, he'd missed the connection he wanted on the chip by less than a millimeter. Gritting his teeth, he moved the wire.

Agony shot through his arm again, but he could feel the bare tip of the wire contact the chip's data port. The chip locked onto it, and he could let go. He wiped the blood off his shaking fingers onto his pants. He was a mess, but that was the least of his concerns right now. Before his courage failed him, he gripped the second wire, estimated the location of the second port on the chip, and stabbed himself again.

His wrist was hurting so badly that the second wound barely added to the pain. Again, he probed the wire about until it locked on to the port. Then, gasping for breath and trying to contain his screams, he moved back to the flitter's engine compartment. He was dripping blood everywhere, but that wasn't bothering him.

Let anyone who wanted his DNA get as much as they liked. He just wanted the pain to be over as quickly as possible.

But first, he was going to add to it.

He connected the first wire to the battery. Then he hesitated a second, anticipating further agony. Knowing that he had no choice, he tapped the battery with the end of the second wire.

Fire burned through his wrist, and this time he couldn't contain his screams. He howled in pain and dropped the wire. He could smell the burning of his wrist, and heat seared from the inside. Tears streaming down his face, he collapsed onto the roadway, consumed by the pain.

Gradually, the fire burned down, and he could start thinking again. His breath was coming in short, spastic gasps as he sat up. His wrist felt as if it had been crushed. It took him two attempts with his left hand to pick up the monitor and hold it over his bleeding, injured wrist. It showed that his plan had worked — his IC was well and truly dead. He knew how it must feel. Swallowing hard, he reached down and jerked the two wires out of his wrist again. Then he wrapped a cloth around his bleeding arm.

He hadn't punctured any vital veins, at least. The bleeding should stop eventually. The pain, too, he hoped. He needed medical aid, but he didn't dare to go to a hospital. Faced with a nonfunctioning chip, the doctors would definitely call a shield. Tristan would have to cope as best as he could on his own. Maybe he could find a store with medical supplies somewhere. . . .

Though with his chip not working, how could he buy anything?

As soon as he could stand, he slung his pack across his shoulder and staggered across to the corpse of the nearest thug. Tristan was glad he hadn't eaten for hours. He doubted if he could have kept anything down right now. The man was missing part of one leg, and his skull had been smashed open. Tristan avoided looking at the drying liquids that had spilled from the body. Focusing only on the man's wrist, he started to work.

As quickly as possable, he extracted the man's IC and cleaned it off as best he could. Then he took a small box from his pack, and placed the chip into it. Finally, he took small skin samples from the man and placed them into a second box.

Lastly, he checked the man's pockets for any clues as to who he might have been. Nothing, of course. A hundred years ago, he would have carried a wallet and identification cards of a dozen different kinds. But all of the money and ID he'd ever have needed were on his chip.

Tristan realized that he'd pushed his luck just as far as it could go. Staggering to his feet again, he turned his back on the wreckage, the corpses, his home, and — in short — his entire past. With the destruction of his IC, Tristan had effectively wiped himself out. He could never again access his old identity. It was as if Tristan Connor no longer existed.

And, considering everything, maybe that wasn't such a bad thing. . . .

Genia was scared and furious, in equal measures. Scared, because she was now in the legal system. She wasn't entirely sure what that meant from the inside. But she was certain that it didn't mean anything good for her. It was all very efficient and very impersonal.

The fury came from the humiliation of it all. Even forgetting for a moment that she had been lied to and betrayed — which she couldn't, of course; it hurt far too much to simply forget about it — they were treating her like an animal being led to slaughter. Nobody explained anything to her; they simply gave her orders, and expected them to be obeyed.

Like with her clothing. She'd been forced to remove all of her own expensive, stylish clothes, and had been given in their place a simple one-piece outfit. It covered all of her body, arms and legs, and fastened shut by simply running her hand down the seam. But it was made (deliberately?) rough, and it chafed her skin wherever it touched. If she sat down, she had to stay still to avoid rubbing herself raw. If she moved, she had to move carefully, or the cloth acted like a file on her flesh.

She'd protested, of course, but the shield hadn't been interested. "You're a criminal," the woman replied. "You've chosen to reject society. Don't expect favors from us."

"I'm an *accused* criminal," Genia retorted. "I haven't even had my trial yet."

"That's next," the officer said flatly. She showed neither interest nor irritation; she was simply doing her duty. At least Shimoda had shown some individuality and fire!

The outfit was a dull brown. It did nothing for her appearance. Genia hated it, but she literally had nothing else to wear.

Her cell inspired similar feelings. It was tiny, only three paces in any direction. There was a small shelf for a bed, a sink, and a toilet. Nothing to do, nothing to read. She simply had to sit and wait. Genia considered complaining, but she had a strong suspicion she knew what answer she'd get. In the end, she waited only an hour before the policewoman returned for her.

"The judge will see you now," she said, opening the cell door. "Come on."

"That's fast," Genia answered. Despite being a victim of the system, she had to admire its speed.

"We want you out of here," the woman replied. "Follow me." She led the way down the corridor and into the courtroom. Genia briefly considered making an escape attempt, but what was the point? She was in shield headquarters, and even if she got away from her escort, there had to be many more officers around.

The courtroom wasn't a great deal larger than her cell. There was a high bench, at which a stern-looking woman sat — presumably the judge — and a smaller table at which two other people sat. One had a small bag with him. The other a hand-comp. There was a recording device on the bench, and another small table where the shield directed Genia to stand. The shield took her place behind Genia's back, out of direct sight.

"The court reviewing the case of Genia Doe," the hand-comp man said. "Step forward to be scanned."

Genia frowned. "I don't have an IC," she answered.

That didn't seem to please the judge. She leaned forward. "Are you from the Underworld?"

"Yes," Genia said, defiantly. "It's not my fault, so don't blame me for it."

"Underworld scum," the judge muttered. "Coming up here to loot and pillage."

"Oh, great!" Genia glared at the woman. "I can see I'm going to get a really fair trial here! You're prejudiced against me."

"What I believe is irrelevant to the case," the judge said. She looked at the hand-comp man. "What are the charges?"

"That she's a thief, your honor," he answered.

"What a surprise." The judge rolled her eyes. "Very well, begin."

Genia growled. "Aren't you supposed to present a list of exact charges, or something?" she asked. All she knew about trials came from the occasional vid drama, but in those people always were accused of specific crimes, and the prosecution had to prove the crimes had been committed by the accused. "And aren't I allowed a lawyer or something?"

"Somebody's been watching too much vid," the judge said. "They aren't realistic, you know." She nodded at the second man. "Go on."

The man stood up, taking an intro-dermal from his pack. Genia was very alarmed by now.

"What's going on?" she demanded.

"Truzac," the judge explained with a sigh. "There's

no need for anything else. You will be given the dose and then you will talk. That's it."

"You can't do that to me!"

"Of course we can. What did you think a trial *was*?" The judge gestured, and the man moved toward her.

Genia tried to run, but the shield grabbed her from behind and slammed her against the table. Genia was winded and hurt by the unexpected blow, and before she could fight free, the man had injected the serum into her neck. She yelled wordlessly, and the shield let her go. Genia stood up and her head spun. She grabbed the edge of the table, barely able to remain standing.

"Now," the judge said, her voice all distorted and warbling. "Are you a thief?"

No, Genia tried to say. "Yes," she heard her own voice reply.

"How many times have you stolen?" the judge asked.

Don't answer! Genia screamed soundlessly at herself. Her traitor voice ignored the advice. "I don't remember exactly," she heard herself say. "Over a hundred times, at least." *Thanks a lot!* Genia complained, giving in. There was nothing she could do with the drug in her system.

"Do you feel any remorse for what you have done?" The judge leaned forward, intent on this answer.

Grovel! Genia told herself. *Beg for mercy! Say you'll never do it again!* "None at all," her voice replied, ignoring everything Genia wanted to say.

"Then that is all," the judge said. "It is my finding that you are guilty as charged. You are convicted by your own admissions, and will be removed from society for the good of society as a whole."

Genia tried talking without being questioned. Despite her fuzzy head, she had no problem. "What does that mean?"

"You will be put on Ice for a period of at least ten years," the judge explained. "At the end of that time, if you show remorse for what you have done, you will be freed." The judge paused, and then added, "The remorse will have to be shown under Truzac, of course."

Of course. No pretended reformations here! Genia sagged, not from the effects of the drug, but because of what this meant. She would be locked away for ten years, without contact with the outside world. Somehow she didn't think they'd allow her to use the Net. "You might as well just kill me," Genia said angrily. "What will I do for those ten years?"

"You are meant to consider what you've done and repent your crimes," the judge told her. "You should think that other people your age are dating, having boyfriends, working toward useful and pleasant careers, shopping the NetMalls, taking Virtual Vacations, and enjoying themselves. By your actions, you have chosen not to be a part of that world."

"You stupid hypocrite!" Genia screamed. "I'm from the *Underworld*! I was never given a chance at any of those things. My father was sent to jail, and my mother died when I was a child. I had to fight every single day simply to stay alive! If I'd had the chance at the life you mentioned, I probably would never have stolen. But I didn't. All I knew was that I'd been thrown aside like garbage by people who thought they were somehow better than me. And now you're blaming me because I stole to survive! And you try and call this *justice*?"

"It *is* justice," the judge said. "You stole. The reasons are immaterial. Now you will be punished for it." Abruptly, she smiled. "In a way, I'm doing you a favor. On Ice, you don't need to fight to survive. All you need will be given you. It will be better than the life you knew."

"No, it won't," Genia snapped. "For one thing, I won't be free. For another, I won't be on the Net, will I?"

"Of course not. That is where you stole. We cannot allow you access to such a powerful tool. You will be allowed books, and a Screen to watch vid dramas. And you will be able to talk to your fellow prisoners. That is all, until you show genuine repentance."

Genia's heart sank. She knew that she would never regret what she had done. People like this heartless autocrat deserved whatever Genia could do to them. How could Genia ever come to feel guilty for surviving?

She knew that at the end of ten years she'd fail the examination, and be sent back. If it was up to the system, she'd never get out of jail — ever.

6

Inspector Shimoda groaned, rubbed her temples, and pushed herself away from the Terminal. She had been working too long, and her eyes were hurting. She had a low-level headache starting. And she had managed to get herself almost exactly nowhere. She grabbed her coffee cup and then realized that it was stone-cold. The coffee in it was scummed over. Disgusted, she threw it out and got herself a fresh cup. She needed a break for a while.

All she had managed to do was to become more aware of how sophisticated the guard dogs were. She was no slouch as a programmer, but whoever had created these was far superior to her. They had Tristan's mark all over them, so she knew it had to be him. Just like the Doomsday Virus itself.

There was no sign of Tristan being arrested yet. She checked the logs and discovered that he had somehow escaped from the Worth home after the alert was sounded. That had been several hours ago, and there were no further reports. Well, he was a bright kid — he had to know that the police were after him. He'd probably planned for it and gone to ground somewhere. Shimoda was annoyed at that, but there was nothing much she could do about it right now. Until he surfaced, or some new clues turned up, he was obviously well-hidden. But he'd make a mistake sooner or later, and then she would have him.

She looked out of the window at the blankness outside. It took her a moment to realize that night had fallen. There were lights close by, but over the river Manhattan was still without power. Temporary lights had been set up for the use of rescue workers, but the city itself was still dead. She realized that she hadn't checked on how things were in Manhattan for hours. One of her friends was operating a switchboard, so Shimoda asked her how it was going.

"Rough," the woman replied. "Rescue teams have managed to get out several thousand people, most of whom are in shock. They've been transferred to special areas, where they are fed and given beds. But this is a major disaster. Several thousand are dead, and if you look closely you can see that some fires are still burning. New York is finished, Taki. Even if they can get rid of the virus and get the computers back on-line, the city will never be the same. And those poor people . . . their entire lives have been erased. Their credit history, their personal information, their homes — all gone. It's going to take years to get them back to where they once were. This criminal of yours has destroyed tens of thousands of lives."

"We'll get him," Shimoda promised grimly. "He won't get away with what he's done. I'll put him on Ice for the rest of his life — and beyond, if I can." She was too tired to feel any real emotion other than determination. But it would be very easy to hate Tristan Connor. She sipped her coffee. "I've taken up enough of your time," she apologized. "I'll talk to you later."

She walked back to the window. Her friend was right; you could still see some buildings burning across the river. People were dying, and others were being rescued by the dedicated teams. Shimoda turned back to her Terminal. This was a scene that would be repeated over and over again if she couldn't work out some way to stop that Doomsday Virus. Only, in the rest of the world there would be no rescue units. They would be as disabled as New York was. If the virus escaped, *everything* would cease to work.

Shimoda knew she wasn't ready to get back to work yet. Her mind wouldn't be able to focus. Instead, she thought about Genia. She felt terribly guilty about the poor kid. The girl had come to her for help, and Shimoda had let her down. True, it wasn't really her fault — Peter Chen, after all, had been the one to give the orders to have Genia arrested and tried — but that didn't help soothe Shimoda's conscience. There should have been something she could have done to help the girl. She was technically a thief, but how else could she have survived all those years in the Underworld? If she'd been born into a good family instead, Genia would most likely have become a very productive member of society. As it was, she'd never had a chance.

Shimoda logged into the shield records and saw that Genia had already been tried and convicted. She was due to be shipped off to Ice in the morning. Shimoda briefly wondered about going to visit the girl, but rejected the idea. It would do neither of them any good at all. There was nothing Shimoda could do to make Genia feel any better, and seeing her would only make Shimoda feel worse.

If only Chen hadn't ordered her arrest!

Something suddenly struck Shimoda. She stood still, stunned.

How had Chen known that Genia was a thief?

Shimoda went over what she had done and said to her boss. She had never once mentioned the girl, except to say that Genia was helping her. She hadn't filed a report about Genia asking for protection — though, technically, she should have. And Genia certainly didn't have a record of any kind. How had Chen known who she was?

The inspector shuddered. She had realized by now, of course, that there were people in the police who had to be working with this Quietus project. The presence of the clone of Borden, one of Computer Control's most private people, proved that. And those thugs that she had saved Tristan Connor from were tapped into shield channels. So, there were dcfinitely leaks.

Was *Chen* one of those leaks? Shimoda didn't like that thought at all. She and her boss had very different operating styles, and frequently argued about her actions. He was stubborn, shortsighted, and pigheaded. But she didn't want to believe that he was a traitor, too.

Yet how else could she explain how he knew about Genia? Aside from herself, only Quietus knew who Genia was. The girl had stolen a sample of the Doomsday Virus and then been targeted for death because of it. If Chen hadn't learned of Genia from Shimoda, then he *must* have learned about her from Quietus.

And that was a very scary thought. . . .

What could Shimoda do about this? She could hardly confront him with her accusation. He'd not only be bound to deny it, but if he *was* with Quietus he'd undoubtedly want to remove Shimoda from the picture. He couldn't afford to have anyone know of accusations against him. So confronting him was out of the question — if he was innocent, it wouldn't help. And if he was guilty, she might as well shoot herself in the head.

No. She needed proof, one way or the other, about him. Then she could go to van Dreelen, who was in overall charge of the police department. He'd certainly act if one of his subordinates was a traitor. But for that, Shimoda would need airtight evidence.

Feverishly, she started another search engine operating on her Terminal. This one would check out everything she could discover about Peter Chen.

It was her only hope of staying alive. . . .

One thing that Jame Wilson never tired of was the view from the main observation room. The whole exterior wall was of triple-reinforced synth-glass. Three meters tall and ten meters long, it opened straight out onto the

Martian surface. The colony was nestled near Syrtis Major, and the window looked out toward the Utopian Plain. The redness of the soil was astonishing, and not uniform at all. There were rust-reds, and deep reds; some shades were more like magenta, while others were the color of blood. The thin atmosphere of the planet tinged the sky with pinkish-red. Jame liked to come here every morning, straight after breakfast, before he had to start school. It was a wonderful reminder that he was one of the fortunate people who was helping to shape the future of Mars. He was much more fortunate than fourteen-year-old kids on Earth.

Of course, *they* could go for a walk outside their homes without having to get into an environmental suit and attach oxygen tanks to their backs. The atmosphere on Mars was so thin, you might as well be living in a vacuum as far as most things were concerned. But Jame considered that a small price to pay for the tremendous opportunity ahead of him: creating a new world where people could live and grow.

Jame was even better off than most of the other two hundred kids on Mars because his father was the second most powerful man there. Charle Wilson was the deputy administrator for the planet, a position of tremendous responsibility and power. This gave Jame a wonderful view of what was actually happening on Mars, and filled him with excitement.

Grinning happily, Jame headed from the observation room, and hurried toward his father's office. Mars only had a third of the gravity of Earth, so he had to be careful not to go too fast — he could bump his head on the ceiling if he got carried away! The colony was a busy place, and people waved in friendly greeting as he passed them. Since there were only six hundred people here, apart from the children, Jame actually knew quite a few of them. Those he didn't know were still pretty friendly. In a place like this, you had to get along — or get out.

His father's office was quite small, considering he was such a powerful man. But there wasn't room to waste here yet, and Mr. Wilson wasn't at all concerned about the trappings of power. Jame's mother was also his father's assistant, but she wasn't in yet. She was taking Jame's kid sister, Fai, to nurture school before starting work. Jame went through her cubiclelike office and tapped on the inner door before entering.

His father looked up from his work with a frown. The room contained only his desk, a Terminal and Screen, and a couple of chairs. There was no window, since it was twenty meters underground — for protection against radiation — and only a strip light illuminated the tiny office. Mr. Wilson tried to smile when he saw Jame, but Jame could tell that it was forced.

"Bad day, huh, Dad?" he asked, sympathetically.

"Politics," his father replied, running a hand through his hair and closing down his Screen for the moment. "It's the worst cuss word I know. But it's nothing for you to concern yourself with. It'll all work out, I'm sure. It always does."

Jame nodded. He knew that there was always some new problem to be solved, and sometimes it couldn't be done the simplest and most obvious of ways. Between the various political parties, the workers' unions, and the regulations imposed by Earth, sometimes compromises had to be found. And it usually fell on his father's shoulders to keep everyone at least partially happy.

"Well, I'm off to school," Jame said. "I just wanted to say hello first."

"I appreciate it, son." His father shook his head. "Some days I think I must have been insane to bring my family to this planet."

Jame was shocked. "Don't say that, Dad!" he gasped. "I love it here! I wouldn't want to be growing up on Earth."

"But if you did, you'd have access to better Terminals," his father pointed out. "You'd be part of EarthNet, and able to take school at home like a normal kid, instead of having to go to a special building." He sighed. "Well, once MarsNet is up and running, maybe we can enter the twenty-first century." He laughed, rather bitterly. "Maybe by the twenty-second!"

"Hey, Dad, it's fine," Jame assured him. "I don't miss anything we had back on Earth at all. Honest, I'm really happy here. And I thought you were, too."

His father sighed again. "Most days I am," he replied. "But some days . . . Well, maybe the day will get better." His phone chimed. "And maybe it won't. Look, son, I think you'd better run along now. I have a feeling this is going to be a real busy day for me."

"Sure, Dad." Jame understood. "See you." He left the office, and heard his father make the connection as the door slid shut behind him. His poor father had so much work to do.

Come to think of it, so did he! Forgetting his father's problems for the moment, Jame hurried off to school.

This game wasn't quite as much fun any longer, and Devon wondered if he really wanted to continue to play. When Quietus had given him unlimited time and access to the computers, it had been great, just to see what he could do. He still had dozens of Screens up, and he was idly watching all kinds of activities on them. His pet family was dull right now; they were all logged on to their computers, and you could only take so much of watching people stare into their cybernetic helmets and occasionally scratch themselves. He switched off those Screens. The rescue efforts in New York were going on, but it was boring to simply watch dead bodies being dragged from their homes. Most of the fires were out, and there were no more spectacular explosions or crashes to see.

He forced himself to turn off the rest of the Screens. This was mildly scary, since he'd never been without Screens for as long as he could recall. He *always* had something running, to see or do. Even when he was asleep, he left them on to awaken to. Now, he was closing things down, shutting off programs, and hiding the access codes.

Tristan, it seemed, was still alive.

He'd been *very* irritated to discover this fact. When his thugs hadn't reported in, he'd checked on their ICs. He'd discovered that two of them had stayed still for a very long time now. The third had moved off after a long delay. Maybe he was injured, maybe he was heading for a hospital. It hardly mattered. If the men had succeeded in killing Tristan, one of them would have reported in.

Devon could find no trace of Tristan. It was *possible* that the boy was dead and vaporized, but not likely. The police had a Shield Priority Alert out on him, and he had been spotted at the house of his girlfriend. Quietus had intervened after Tristan's escape and insisted on the punishment of the entire Worth family. That was smart — to set an example of what might happen to anyone who helped the fugitive.

But that meant Tristan was probably still alive somewhere. And he'd found some way to cover his tracks. Devon was forced to start considering the idea that maybe Tristan was nearly as smart as himself. The boy *was* his clone, after all, and possessed the same capabilities as Devon. Devon's advantage, of course, was his training and his genius. Tristan seemed to be happy to be considered normal, while Devon knew that *he* was exceptional.

Only, it looked as if Tristan was starting to wise up. And that could be very unfortunate. As long as Tristan was alive, Quietus had a hold on Devon. And Devon had managed to annoy the Malefactor because of the mess with the Doomsday Virus . . . the virus that Tristan's dumb guard dogs were keeping trapped, for the moment. . . . This might suit Quietus's plans for the time being, but they would want Devon to destroy the dogs and let loose the virus soon. And Devon didn't know how to do that.

He'd tried analyzing the dogs, but they were horribly elusive. He'd tried attacking them, but they snapped and ran. Devon didn't want to go too far and accidentally destroy them too soon, so he was limited in his approach. That was the only reason the solution hadn't come to him yet.

But the Malefactor was unlikely to accept this reasonable fact as an excuse. Not when he had Tristan around. Given Quietus's contacts in the shields, if Tristan were arrested Quietus would be able to get their hands on him very quickly. And that would make Devon's position more tenuous. . . .

It was definitely time for him to leave quietly. The question was whether Quietus would allow him just to walk out. After all, he was their ultimate weapon at the moment, and the key to their plans. If he were to defect to the other side, he could bring the whole conspiracy tumbling down.

For a moment, Devon considered doing precisely that. Going to Computer Control and telling them everything. It would certainly get him out of trouble, and get the Malefactor and everyone else into hot water. He could cripple Quietus if he tried.

But the thought didn't last long — he had no animosity toward Quietus, and a certain amount of admiration for its members. He'd prefer to simply take it over, rather than destroy it.

Besides, Devon didn't actually know the real names of the people in Quietus. There was a good chance that anyone he went to with an offer to defect would actually be a member of Quietus.

So that was out. What he had to do, then, was to get out of the clutches of the Malefactor and be free. Then he could set up his own operations, reactivate all of his programs, and get to work. After all, Quietus aimed to take over the world. So if he took over Quietus, then *he* would rule the world.

What a game *that* would be!

But first — escape.

He closed down most of the Terminal's functions, locking every piece of data away under his own unbreakable codes. The Terminal was still generating the virus, and only he could shut it off. And he had no intention of doing that.

Now for the escape plan.

First he had to discover where he actually was. Devon blinked as he realized that he didn't have any idea where he was living. He'd never bothered with it before because it hadn't been important. In his suite of rooms he had anything he wished for, and if anything wasn't here he simply ordered it and it came. He'd never had any need or desire to leave, except by telepresence. Now that he thought about it, it was actually rather thrilling — to discover where he was!

He moved to the outside door, and activated the sub-Terminal there. If he was correct, then Quietus wouldn't *want* him ever to leave. There would be some kind of "present" there to prevent him from —

Ah! There it was! A small, hidden subroutine . . . If Devon activated the door, a nonlethal but very nasty electrical shock would pass through it — and him.

Devon deactivated the program. It was childishly simple.

Too simple? Devon grinned. If he had set the traps, he'd have nestled several together. Quietus didn't have anyone else as brilliant as him, but it was really unlikely that they'd set only one trap to keep him in place. . . .

Trap two was hidden inside the routines of trap one. By zeroing out the charge, Devon had activated the second trap. This was a lethal blast of power that would release if he touched the door. Devon deactivated that one, and checked for a third.

And there it was — an alarm circuit to a small House-bot in the next section of the building. One with a staser set to incapacitate anyone exiting the rooms. Devon whistled to himself as he rewrote this routine and had the robot shoot itself instead. He liked that little dramatic touch of having the 'bot commit suicide.

Trap four? Yes, there it was . . . a second Housebot, this one programmed to tear Devon's head off. Well, turnabout was fair play. . . . He made the 'bot rip its own head off and stomp it to bits. Really, these little games were quite obvious. Couldn't they manage anything more subtle?

Yes, he discovered, they could. Trap nine was a beauty. By the time he'd gone that far, he was getting bored, and this one perked him up again. It was simple enough — anybody stepping out into the corridor caused all of the air to be sucked out of the vents, so Devon would be asphyxiated. The sneaky bit was when he rewrote it, because it automatically reversed all of his changes. If he hadn't been so careful and smart, he would have thought he'd taken the trap off-line, when it had simply snuck behind him, rewriting itself.

This was a good one! Devon was enjoying it. What he did then was swiftly to write another program and turn it loose. Then Devon went to work rewriting trap nine. The original program started to rewrite itself, as it had planned. Devon's new program then crept in and started unwriting the program. Which started to rewrite itself again . . .

Trapped inside a logical loop, the program kept dying and recreating itself forever. While it was doing that, it couldn't monitor Devon himself. Tricky! That one had been a lot of fun. It had also apparently been the final trap. Devon was almost insulted that Quietus had believed nine was enough. Oh, well, they'd learn — now that it was too late.

He tapped the code to open the door, and stepped outside. For a second he held his breath. Had he been right? Or were there more traps?

He proceeded down the corridor, stepping over the wreckage of the first destroyed 'bot. The second was still busy stomping on its head, and ignored him. As he stepped out of the corridor, he realized he'd been right about the traps.

And he stopped, astonished.

He really hadn't any idea where he lived, of course, but he'd had expectations. Probably somewhere near New York, he thought, since that was where his virus had struck. Maybe in another major city. But he had never even considered *this*.

Ahead of him was a crowded concourse. People were moving everywhere, all with their own purposes. Some carried equipment, others packages. Some were in uniforms, others in street clothing. It was a busy scene Devon had seen thousands of times before, in malls or airports or other areas where people actually had to be physically present.

What made this scene different was the number of windows in the background. The view through most of them was, for all intents and purposes, identical.

Stars.

Only, out of three windows, close together, Devon could see part of Earth. Clouds covered up most of it, but he could make out a portion of Australia.

He wasn't anywhere at all on Earth — he was in orbit.

He lived on Overlook, the space station!

7

Mora sat, her face in her hands, utterly depressed. This had been the worst day of her life. Everything had gone so wrong, and she had no idea when this dreadful slide of events would end. Here she was, in a cell, of all places. She had her clothes, but everything else had been taken from her. She couldn't even comb her hair. And she'd been left here for several hours, not even offered food or drink.

She didn't care. Nothing mattered now. Her whole life was a shambles. She'd been bitterly humiliated. All of her friends would hear about this, and they'd never talk to her again. And Tristan had betrayed her, killing all of those people. Then he'd somehow escaped when she had tried to get help for him, and she'd been blamed for it. How could things get any worse?

A female shield rapped on the bars of her cell. "Come on," the woman said gruffly. "The judge will see you now."

"Are they letting me go?" Mora asked eagerly.

"How should I know?" the shield grumbled. "They don't tell me any more than I need to know to do my job. Come on."

Mora was led to a small courtroom. The judge was there, a thin-faced, grim woman behind her desk, glaring down. There were two men there — and her parents, both with shields of their own. Mora tried to greet them, but the police woman tapped her roughly on the shoulder.

"You talk only when the judge allows it," the woman said sternly.

"Thank you," the judge said, glaring down at Mora. "You are Mora Worth, daughter of Hal and Welma Worth?"

"Yes, ma'am," Mora said, politely. It wouldn't hurt to impress the woman with her manners. She glanced around. "But . . . where's Marka?" The police woman used a rod, which sent a sharp electrical charge through her arm, making her yelp. She'd forgotten she wasn't supposed to talk.

"You are all accused of aiding a wanted felon, Tristan Connor. Evidence from the police officers present at your house has been deposited with the court and confirms that Connor was in your house and then released by the private code of the Worth family. One of you therefore is guilty of helping him escape. The rest of you are guilty of allowing this to happen and not turning over the criminal for instant justice."

Mr. Worth looked stunned. "That's preposterous!" he exclaimed. The shield behind him zapped him, and made Mora's father cry out in pain.

"You will speak only when asked a question or given permission to speak!" the judge informed him. "You have all been found guilty of obstructing a police investigation. Given the status of your family in the community, this is unforgivable. To set an example to anyone else who might consider helping wanted criminals evade capture, you are to be severely punished."

The judge glared at Mora. "The younger daughter, Marka, is considered too young to be held responsible for her actions. She has accordingly been placed in the custody of an aunt, where she will remain. The rest of you are old enough to take the consequences of your deeds. It is the judgment of this court that you be stripped of your membership in society and that you are to be exiled for the remainder of your lives to the Underworld."

Mora couldn't believe what she had just heard. "But, your honor —" she began, dazed and horrified. Then she was shocked hard and fell forward. She yelled in pain, and clutched the edge of the table to support herself.

"This is an outrage!" her father yelled, before he, too, was stunned. Her mother said nothing; tears trickled down her cheeks, and she went white.

This can't be happening! Mora stood up, her back hurting where she had been zapped. She knew better than to speak again, though. She fought back tears, refusing to let these monsters see her cry. *How can they do this to me?* she wondered.

"Sentence is to be carried out immediately," the judge announced. One of the seated men rose. He had a small instrument in his hand, and he moved to stand before Mora.

"Hold out your right arm," he ordered. Mora knew she had no option but to obey. The man gripped her wrist and fitted his tool over it like a sleeve. "This may hurt a bit," he said, almost apologetically.

That was an understatement. Pain flared through her

wrist, and she cried out. He held her firmly, and she felt some sort of chemicals being pumped into her arm that deadened the pain completely. Numbly, she stood there until the machine bleeped and he removed it and went on to her mother.

Mora rubbed her unfeeling wrist, and saw that there was a small scar on it, already starting to heal. For a moment she didn't know what it was. And then the truth hit her with an emotional blow harder than any of the physical ones she had suffered.

They had removed her IC!

She was without access to the Net. She had no way of shopping, or talking to people. She had no access to her accounts or her identity.

She was *nobody*!

With a cry of shock, she collapsed. The shield grabbed her, hauling her back to her feet without sympathy. In a daze, Mora watched as her mother and then her father were both given the same treatment.

The judge seemed determined to rub it in. "You have turned your back on your society by harboring a criminal," she informed them coldly. "Your society has now turned its back on you in return. Take them away."

The three shields grabbed them roughly and dragged

them from the room. Mr. Worth yelled out, "This wasn't a trial! I know my rights! I want to be given Truzac!"

The shield hauling her father punched him. "Shut up, scum!" he snapped. "You don't have any rights! You're *nothing*, understand? If I were to kill you right now, nobody would care. So don't get me angry, understand?"

That seemed to get through to Mr. Worth, and he shut up. Mora didn't know enough about the law to say if what they had suffered was normal or not. All she knew was that her entire life was over.

Numbly, she sat in the shield flitter as it took the three of them away from the court. She barely noticed where they were going, but finally the flitter dropped to a landing and the doors opened. One of the shields got out. They were close to a building, and there was a sort of trapdoor in the roadway in front of it. The shield passed his wrist over the locking mechanism, and then tapped in a code.

The trapdoor opened upward, revealing the top of a ladder. The shield turned to the flitter and gestured. The policewoman with Mora punched her on the arm. "Out," she ordered. Her arm stinging from the blow, Mora sullenly obeyed. Her parents climbed out behind her.

"That's it," the head shield said, gesturing down at

the ladder. "Down you go." He almost smiled. "And you won't ever be coming back up. This door locks behind you, and won't open for you again."

"But what will we do?" Mrs. Worth cried. "How will we live?"

"That's up to you to figure out," the shield answered. "But, if I were you, I'd find somewhere to hide pretty fast. They're not civilized down there, you know."

"You can't do this to us!" Mr. Worth exclaimed, standing up straight. "I know my rights! I am an important officer of Jacoby and Stern! I have the right to a fair trial, not that —" He howled as the shield punched him in the stomach.

"Understand this," the man said. "You have *no* rights. You have *nothing*! You've been sent to the Underworld, and that's it. Now, either climb down there or I'll push you over the edge myself. You have five seconds."

Mora could see that the shield wasn't kidding; he was really ready to push her father over the edge. She glanced down, and saw the drop was at least thirty feet, maybe as much as fifty. It would kill him. Mora had no option now but to do what she could to save his life. With a horrible feeling of dread and disgust, she started down the ladder.

"Smart girl," she heard the shield say. "Now, you two — down."

Mora didn't look back, too afraid that she'd burst into tears. Nor did she have the courage to look down at what her new life would be. Instead, she stared straight ahead as she climbed down. All she could see were the old gray walls of some long-forgotten building. Above her, she heard her parents get onto the ladder and start down.

Then, with a final clang, the trapdoor was shut, and she heard it sealed.

With that, most of the light was gone. There was only a faint glow from below, barely enough for her to see her hands. She could see nothing else, except the vague suggestion of rungs as she kept descending. She steeled herself to feel nothing, but she could feel the tears trickling down her cheek.

Her life was over, no matter what happened now.

Then her feet touched ground; she stumbled away from the ladder a few paces and waited for her shaken parents to join her. Her mother clutched Mora and burst into tears.

"It's dark and filthy, Hal," she moaned. "What are we going to do?"

Mr. Worth shook his head. Mora could barely see it.

"I don't know. I don't have any idea what we *can* do. I'd never thought about this place before today. I have no idea what's possible down here."

"Will we die?" Mora asked him.

Her father sighed — though it almost sounded like a sob. "It's possible," he confessed. "I know I should tell you that I'll work something out, and that everything will be fine. But who can say whether it will be."

"I can," said a fresh voice, and suddenly there was a light turned on them. It probably wasn't very bright, really, but in the gloom it looked like a searchlight. Mora gasped as the figure holding the flashlight stepped forward and looked at them. He was tall, skinny, and dressed almost entirely in gray. He looked as if he might have been made from the bricks and stones of the buildings behind him. "My name's Barker," he added. "And you three are new arrivals, aren't you? No clue what to do, how to survive?"

Mr. Worth protectively moved closer to Mora and her mother. "What do you want?" he asked. Even Mora could hear the fear in his voice.

"We're all in the same boat down here," Barker said. "Castoffs from Above. We have to work together if we're going to survive. I've been down here most of my life, and I can teach you the lessons you'll need to be able to eat and live down here."

"That's very kind of you," Mr. Worth answered, relaxing slightly. He'd obviously been afraid that there would be a fight.

Mora wasn't so sure. "What's in this for you?" she demanded.

Barker laughed. "Good question, missy. The answer is numbers. There are some people down here who think they can bully the rest of us. But if we band together, we can stand up to the criminal element. It's all a matter of cooperation and trust."

"Quite right," agreed Mr. Worth. He moved toward the light. "I'm really glad we met you, Mr. Barker."

Barker nodded, and Mora decided that she didn't trust him. "I think we should go our own way," she said. "We don't have any reason to trust this man." She'd expected Barker to be annoyed, but he just grinned.

"Smart girl; you don't." The gray man shook his head. "She's got more brains than you." He whistled, and suddenly there were six or seven other men around them. It was hard to count them in the gloom.

It wasn't hard to see the flash of knives, however.

"What are you doing?" Mrs. Worth asked in a strangled voice.

Barker rolled his eyes. "What does it look like?" he asked. "We're robbing you, of course."

"But we have nothing left!" Mr. Worth exclaimed.

Barker snorted. "Typical thinking for someone from Above." He moved forward and grabbed Mr. Worth's arm roughly. "You have these fancy clothes of yours," he said, holding out some ragged blankets. "I think it's time to swap." After they'd gotten what they wanted, the thugs vanished, all save for Barker, who kept the flashlight trained on them.

"I've taken all of your last possessions," he said. "And I've taken one other thing: your innocence. That's a very important lesson."

"But what are we to do now?" Mr. Worth pleaded.

"That's up to you," Barker answered. "Nobody will bother you now. You've got nothing left that anyone wants down here. But if you find anything, remember this lesson well. There will always be someone who will take whatever you have — if he can."

"So you're just leaving us to die?" Mrs. Worth asked.

"No." Barker shook his head, and gestured upward. "Your fine fellow citizens up there left you to do that. I'm leaving you to see if you can live." He looked again at Mora. "If you can, I may be able to use you."

"As what?" she asked him coldly.

"I don't know yet," he admitted. There are possibilities for a smart girl like you, if you want to take them."

"You expect us to *join* you, after what you've done?" Mr. Worth growled.

"Believe me, I've done you a favor," Barker answered. "Most other people would have killed you all. I don't do that. Others might, if they find you. Then you'll realize that this was nothing personal. And if it teaches you a lesson, you might profit by it."

" 'That which does not kill us makes us stronger,' " quoted Mora.

Again Barker looked at her in what seemed like respect. "Bright girl. Don't forget my offer. If you want to join me, I'll know it." He gave them a mock salute with the light, and then it went out.

The darkness seemed even more intense than before. Mrs. Worth whimpered, and her husband put an arm around her. "Those beasts!" he hissed.

"We're going to die!" Mrs. Worth wailed.

Mora pulled the blanket tighter around herself. She was still cold, of course. "No," she said, determination growing. "We won't. We'll survive." She looked at her parents. "But we'd better start learning." She felt inside herself for strength, and fought back the horror, shock, and despair. "Let's find somewhere to hide out. Then we can start thinking about what to do next."

She wasn't going to let them beat her. She *wasn't*. She'd do whatever she had to, to live. And then . . . then she'd work out some way to pay back the people who had done this to her.

Starting with Tristan Connor.

8

If the situation hadn't been so horrible, Tristan might have been enjoying himself. He'd found a library building and had broken in — carefully! — to gain access to one of the computers. Nobody ever bothered actually going to one of these buildings anymore, except for update staff. All books had been scanned into the Net by 2032, and their paper recycled. Only paper schools complained about the loss. What libraries had once done was now simpler and more efficient on-line. So the buildings had mostly been demolished or left for posterity — as if anyone bothered visiting old buildings anymore! But the ones still there had access to the Net, and that was what Tristan badly needed. Since there was nobody else in the building, he wasn't too worried about being found. And since the alarm company that protected the building was based in New York, they couldn't possibly be coming to investigate a break-in, either.

His main worry had been that the IC he'd stolen would register on the police scanners when he went through the doorway. Then he'd discovered something fascinating.

The chip didn't show up on the scans, as all chips were supposed to.

Tristan remembered that when the thugs had come for him the first time, Inspector Shimoda hadn't been able to track them. Now he had discovered why. The chip he'd taken had a small circuit in it that blocked the police scanners. Whoever had a chip like this in his wrist could go anywhere, undetected, but still be able to access the Net.

And not only the Net. Tristan had logged in and checked the dead man's account, downloading all information to his own secret file. He'd set one up earlier under the name "Centrus," and it was now coming in handy. All his old accounts would be monitored, but nobody knew about this one. As he downloaded the dead man's file, Tristan searched for clues.

He found something significant immediately. The man had unlimited credit access. Anything he wanted, he could buy. Useful . . .

He didn't seem to have a name, which was interesting. Nor a job, nor a family. But he had unlimited money and unlimited access, all through the authority of Computer Control itself. Which had to mean one of only two things. First, the man could be a special agent, working for Computer Control. Tristan didn't think this was very likely, since he was working for someone who was trying to break Computer Control. Second, he could be a traitor, working for Quietus while supposedly a government agent. That made a lot more sense.

It also made Tristan's job a lot harder. If there were Quietus agents in Computer Control itself, then he couldn't just contact Control and tell them what was happening. There was no way of knowing if whoever he spoke to was a real person, or worked for Quietus. Not even Inspector Shimoda. True, she'd apparently saved his life when Devon had first struck. But maybe that was only so that she could get closer to him and betray him later.

He couldn't trust *anyone* right now.

What he had to do, first and foremost, was to locate Quietus and stop the virus. To do that, he needed to locate the Terminal that had generated the Doomsday Virus.

Using his Centrus data, he set to work. He didn't pay any attention to anything until he realized that his stomach was growling. Puzzled, he stopped working. How long had it been since he'd last eaten? He couldn't remember. He grabbed a protein bar and a carton of water from the supplies he'd stuck in his pack and ate and drank as he worked.

The library didn't have speedboards. He guessed he was lucky that they had Terminals that weren't too outdated. It meant that his work was all on old-fashioned keyboard, though, which slowed him down. But eventually he started getting somewhere.

Devon's account data started to come up. He'd managed to track back the earlier release of the virus and set old guard dogs after it . . . when? It seemed like weeks ago, but it was only slightly more than a day! His program had kept running, and it was almost ready to report. As he waited, he checked out the Quietus log entries, and discovered that they had been accessed again over the course of the last twenty-four hours. Somebody had been very busy indeed, and it had to be Devon.

Then the search finished, and Tristan had the data he needed.

Overlook.

Devon was based on the Overlook station, high above Earth! Tristan wiped the sweat from his forehead and stared at the information. The address was in a very exclusive residential area on the station. Not many people could afford to live there — most only went up for vacations to the hotels and shops and facilities. The zero-gravity rooms were very popular for sports and play, and the views of Earth were supposed to be magnificent. He'd "visited" Overlook a number of times in Virtual Reality, and loved it.

Now he'd have to do it in person.

This wouldn't be easy. He'd heard that some people got space-sick, and he wondered if it would affect him. He never traveled much, except to visit Mora. Mora . . . He had to avoid thinking about her! Anyway, he'd have to take his chances on getting sick. He *had* to get to Devon's computer.

But how? Physically going into space was something that had never occurred to him before, and he didn't have a clue how to go about it. But that was what the Net was for, after all!

He started hunting, and was pleasantly surprised by the results. There was a daily flight up to Overlook from

Schwarzenegger Spaceport in New Jersey. And it left in the evening, which gave him plenty of time to make it there. Using the dead man's credit, he created a ticket for himself. He couldn't use his real name, but that hardly mattered. He chose "David Flores" instead, picking the name at random from the library's on-line book lists. The stolen chip didn't have a name on it, so he'd be able to get through with a fake name.

Great! While he was at it, he gave himself a window seat. Might as well enjoy the view on the way up! It was a Boeing 343 Ramjet flight, with only forty-three people aboard. It looked like not many people ever wanted to visit Overlook. Or, perhaps, not many could afford to do so.

Now all he had to do was to go to the spaceport. Once again, the chip was the solution. When he put in a call for a flitter, his request was somehow moved automatically to the front of the line. He'd have a pickup in ten minutes.

Tristan grinned. He could almost get to like this business of being a fugitive, as long as he could keep this chip! It was making his life a whole lot easier.

And then a thought struck him: The shields couldn't trace this chip. But that didn't mean *nobody* could. Had Quietus perhaps built in some secret tracking device? If they had, they might know exactly what he had planned by now, and be ready to capture or kill him. . . .

That chilled him. *Did* they know, or was he just being paranoid? After recent events, he hadn't thought it was possible for him to get more scared. He'd been wrong. He was shaking now. Maybe Quietus was allowing him to do all of this just to get him somewhere nice and quiet, like the residence on Overlook, so they could eliminate him without any witnesses.

But — what choice did he have? This *might* be a trap; he had no way of knowing. But if he didn't try it, then the Doomsday Virus would eventually escape and destroy the world as he knew it.

It wasn't even close. This was his only chance to stop the virus cold, and he *had* to take it, no matter how big a risk it was. Tristan made up his mind that he was going through with his plan, come what might.

But almost all of the fun had evaporated now.

Genia's humiliation continued. Her face burning, she was forced to endure it. But she would not forget, and she vowed she would one day get her revenge on each person who contributed to her shaming. She was taken to a small aircraft, one of a private fleet owned and operated by shields in the New York area. Once aboard, she was shackled to a seat in the windowless prisoner area.

"Anyone would think I was Attila the Hun," she complained. "Don't you shields have anything better to do with your time? Like saving New York, or something?"

"Taking care of scum like you is a waste of time, I agree," the female officer watching her admitted. "But, unlike you, I know my duty and I do it. I'm to make sure you're put on Ice, and I'll do it. Gladly."

"Torturer," Genia countered. She rattled her chains. "Is this necessary?"

"There will be no escapes from my custody," the woman replied.

"Can't I even get a window seat?" Genia asked sarcastically.

The shield took her seriously. "There's nothing that you need to see. This will be a lot more pleasant for both of us if you just shut up."

"Yes," growled Genia. "I guess I'm getting to the end of your pleasant chitchat, and your brain's overheating." She sat back, the rough cloth of her jumpsuit irritating her behind. "Don't they have cushions for these things? No, don't tell me — I have no need for comfort."

The shield glared at her. "Keep on irritating me, and I'll decide you don't need toilet paper, either."

"Paper?" Genia rolled her eyes. "This place must be really primitive."

"Then you should feel right at home."

Genia faked looking astonished. "Wow! She *can* crack jokes."

"I can also crack skulls," the woman answered. "I just have to deliver you there. Nobody said you had to be conscious."

Genia could see that she was close to the shield's threat being carried out, so she shut up and paid attention instead. The cabin was sealed, with just the two of them in it, but she could hear the sounds of the aircraft getting ready for takeoff. The various thuds and bumps were doors and hatches closing, and then came the whine of the turbojets and the feeling of motion. Genia had never flown before, and wished that she could see what was happening. To look down on the world from the clouds would be quite something. She'd always enjoyed it on the Net.

Then the plane was in the air, and the hours of boredom set in. It was broken only once when another shield brought food and drink in for Genia and her guard. The food was bland, stewlike stuff, and the drink was plain juice. By that time, though, Genia was hungry enough to eat anything, so she didn't complain. She finished both off, and looked at the plastic spoon she'd been given. Not even a knife, just in case. She could hardly attack the guard with a plastic spoon!

Later she asked to use the toilet, and her request was granted. But the shield stayed with her, which was embarrassing. And there was toilet paper; it really was that primitive.

The little luxuries of life were obviously out.

And then the plane dropped into a descent. Genia's stomach dropped with it, and for a second she thought she'd be sick. But she controlled herself, and endured the landing. A few moments later, the guard unshackled her. Genia rubbed her wrists as she followed the officer out of the cabin.

And into agony.

It was *freezing* outside the plane. Ice and snow lay all around, and a cutting wind ripped right through the thin clothes Genia was wearing. After a minute in which Genia seriously thought she'd freeze to death, the shield threw a blanket around her that cut down most — but not all — of the chill.

"Did you have to wait so long?" Genia demanded, when she could get her frozen jaw working again.

"Yes," the woman answered. "It's to impress upon

you where you now are. This is Antarctica, all around you for hundreds of miles. Take a good look. It might be the last time you see the surface of Earth."

Shivering, the blanket as close as she could clutch it, Genia did so. There was one small building, presumably some sort of control room. And then there was ice and snow, as far as she could see. There was a small vehicle waiting for them, and that was it.

The shield gestured at the vehicle. "That has ten minutes' charge in it," she said. "It can travel to the jail and back, and no farther, without a day's recharging."

"Can't they build something more efficient?" Genia asked.

"They don't want efficiency," the policewoman explained. "Some prisoners imagine they will escape from Ice. Look around you. There's no way to get out of here, so don't even think of escape."

"Actually, right now, I'm thinking of a hot bath and some nice, warm clothes," Genia replied. She was only half-joking.

"Dream on." The shield led her to the vehicle, which was, at least, warm inside. It crawled across the ice and snow to the building. Genia noted that it took almost exactly five minutes. The shields had timed it perfectly. Nobody could use this vehicle to escape in!

She was forced to face the cold outside again to follow the shield to the building's only door. The woman didn't bother looking back to see if Genia was following her; another example of how the police were reinforcing the impossibility of escape.

Inside was split into two sections. One was a bay for the vehicle — meaning that the shield could have driven it in if she'd wanted to, instead of forcing Genia to walk — and the other was an elevator. There was nothing else. The shield tapped the panel for the elevator, and the door opened.

"This is where I get rid of you," the woman said. "Down you go. And don't forget what you've seen."

"I won't forget," Genia said. "And when I get out of here, I won't forget you, either."

"I'm terrified," the shield replied, yawning. "Move."

Genia walked into the elevator, and stood there. The officer tapped in her code, and the doors slid shut. There was a momentary wait, then a stomach-wrenching drop, followed a few seconds later by a nauseating, grinding halt. The door opened again, and Genia looked out to see another shield waiting for her.

"Welcome to Ice," he said. "Your home for at least the next ten years."

Genia stared around, her heart sinking. She stood in a short corridor, hewn from bare rock, and hardly finished except by the addition of light globes to illuminate the place. The shield led her down the corridor and through a door into a reception area. Here at a computer sat a woman who didn't even seem to be interested in Genia. She passed over a wrist-band.

"That's your tag," the shield informed Genia. "There's a small chip in it. Lose it, and you get solitary for a week. It monitors your whereabouts at all times."

Genia slid it on. Maybe for people from Above it might feel comforting. But she'd never had a chip in her life, and this more than anything made her feel like a prisoner. "Now what?" she asked. "My cell, and lock me in?"

"No," the shield replied. He pointed at a door at the end of the room. "You go through there and do whatever you like. Within limits, of course. *Lots* of limits. One of the women will show you where you sleep, and fill you in on the rules, feeding times, and so forth. Other than that, we don't care what you do."

"Gee, thanks." Genia didn't see any point in hanging around where she evidently wasn't wanted. Ignoring the two shields, she marched to the door, which opened as she approached. She walked through, and heard it close again behind her.

Now she was in a larger area. Naturally, there were no windows, but several doors led out of the room. It was about thirty meters long and ten wide, and held tables and chairs. There were about a dozen people in the room, all of them silent and simply sitting still, doing nothing at all. Genia looked around, astonished. This wasn't what she had imagined prison would be like.

"Nobody ever believes what they see when they arrive," a woman's voice said. Genia turned to see a woman leaning against the wall beside the door. She was dressed in slightly better clothing than Genia's, and had a mostly bored expression on her face. She looked as if she were in her mid-thirties.

"I had expected something a little more . . . " Genia groped for the right word.

"Jail-like?" The woman gave a bitter laugh. "Kid, the shields don't care what we do in here. There isn't much they give us." She gestured at the sitting people. "These are the lifers, the ones without hope of release. They have nothing left, so that's just what they occupy themselves with. The rest of us find things to keep us busy."

"You're the person who'll show me where I'm to stay," Genia guessed.

"Right," the woman agreed. "There's only one rule around here, and that's not to ask people questions. If someone wants you to know something, they'll tell you. Otherwise, stay out of matters."

"Matters?"

"That's a question." There was no humor in the woman's voice. "You'll learn. Come on." She led the way through the room.

Genia shuddered as she passed close to one of the lifers. The man was unkempt, his beard untrimmed, and he had a distinct body odor. Obviously bathing was something he'd given up. Genia was about to ask about this, and then remembered the woman's rule. She wondered what her name was, but knew better than to ask. She wondered if the woman knew what Genia's name was — or if she even cared.

As they neared the end of the room, a tall, gray-haired man hurried in. His eyes narrowed as he saw Genia and her escort, and he moved to block their way. "Are you Genia?" he demanded.

Genia glanced at the woman. "That's a question," she grumbled. "He's broken the rule."

"*He's* allowed to," the woman replied. "Answer him."

"Why should I?" These people were obnoxious, and

she saw absolutely no reason why she should cooperate with them at all.

"Because if your name *is* Genia," the man answered, "then I'm your father."

Genia simply stood there, staring at the man she had never known. Her *father* . . .

9

Tristan was surprised and pleased by Schwarzenegger Spaceport. It was bustling, though not overly large. Few enough people bothered to physically move around when you could work just as effectively in Virtual Reality, so the spaceport didn't have to be very large to accomodate those few people who actually did need to go places. There was just the one main building, with large wings radiating out in a star pattern. On these wings were the gates where passengers met their transport. Of the six wings, five were for aircraft, and three of those were for shipping only. Only two wings dealt with air travelers, and neither was terribly busy.

The last wing was for space travel. Most of the larger craft, of course, left from Earth's orbit. You couldn't have nuclear-powered vessels lifting off from crowded living areas, so they were now built and operated in space. Besides, it was a lot cheaper to fly them only in space — they didn't have to stand up to the stresses of landing and taking off from planets. They would have been much heavier if they had to stand up to the gravitational pull of worlds like Earth or Mars. Instead, the big ships that traveled the solar system stayed forever in space, docking at stations like Overlook. Shuttles made the journeys up and down.

Tristan headed for his shuttle, the Delta Ramjet, one of the latest built by Boeing. The other passengers were mostly aboard, because Tristan had deliberately left his own boarding until almost takeoff time. He didn't want to have to sit around and maybe be recognized. It was possible that the police had put out his picture on the Net, after all. They might even have alerted the airlines that he was considered a fugitive, and blocked the airport.

They might even be waiting here for him. . . .

It was a chance he simply had to take. The only way for him to clear his name was to get absolute proof that Devon existed. Otherwise, the evidence implicated him as the maker and deliverer of the Doomsday Virus. And the only place he could get that proof, as well as stop the virus, was on Overlook.

Maybe the shields would believe him if he told them the story. Maybe they would even check Overlook and find the Terminal. But it wouldn't help, because only Tristan or Devon could shut it down. And Devon wouldn't.

The scariest thought was that Tristan would finally come face-to-face with the person from whom he had been cloned. What would he do then? Devon had tried to kill him twice already — he was almost certain to try again. Tristan wished he had a staser or something, but he would never have been able to get it past spaceport security. He was forced to confront his deadly twin unarmed. . . .

Walking through the boarding area was simple compared to that.

As it was, nobody seemed at all bothered by him. The girl behind the check-in desk smiled at him as she confirmed his ticket, and then gestured for him to go aboard. Holding his pack, Tristan walked down the short tube and into the Ramjet. He was glad he'd bought a ticket off to himself by a window. He didn't want to be too close to the other passengers, just in case.

They didn't bother with him anyway. Many were using

their wrist-comps or hand-comps, and were oblivious to whatever was happening around them. A cheerful steward directed Tristan to his seat — the one beside him was empty, which was what he'd planned. Tristan strapped himself in and waited for takeoff.

A moment later, the in-ship communications came on. "Welcome to Delta's shuttle to Overlook," the woman's voice said. "I'm your pilot, Captain O'Hara. Our flying time today should be six hours and fifteen minutes. No problems with wind, of course." She chuckled. "At least, not after the first fifteen minutes, by which time we will have left Earth's atmosphere. So we anticipate a smooth ride. For those concerned, the current problems in New York have not affected our computers. I'll hand you over to the stewards now, who will explain emergency procedures in the remote case we may need to abandon the ship."

Tristan hadn't considered the virus. If it should break free while he was on the shuttle, the craft could crash and burn. And he'd be dead.

He glanced at the front of the cabin, where a young, pretty woman was demonstrating how to put on the seat restraints. Obvious stuff, really. "In case of emergencies, there are four escape hatches which will open automatically, one at the front, one at the rear, and one over each wing," she added. "Once we are in flight, of course, these will be locked. In case of an emergency landing, on land or sea, they will be unlocked and chutes deployed.

"In the event of trouble in the air or in space itself, the alarms will sound. Go immediately to the escape pod closest to your seat. It is important that you go to the closest, because each can only take ten people. Colored strips in the floor will guide you to the correct pod. Your own color is indicated by the flash on the arm of your seat. Look at it now." Tristan's was red.

"Each pod has air for twelve hours," the stewardess continued. "If ejected in the atmosphere, they will parachute to Earth. If ejected into space, they will use small jets to move away from the damaged shuttle. In neither case should anyone aboard the pods attempt to open the hatches. These will be opened by specialist rescue officers. The pods have homing beacons to allow them to be recovered well before oxygen reserves give out. If anyone has any specific questions, please ask a steward. These instructions are also downloaded into your seat-comps, set into the back of the chair in front of you. Please take a moment to scan them."

Tristan didn't bother, because everything seemed to be straightforward enough. Instead, he logged on to see if there was any further news about New York City. He wanted to assess his chances of reaching Overlook safely. He'd barely scrolled past the obligatory politicians claiming that everything was being handled, when the Screen blanked out.

"This is Captain O'Hara," the Screen said. "Prepare for takeoff. All Screens must be shut down until I give the all clear."

One steward checked that Tristan had his restraints fastened, and then moved on. Tristan glanced out of the window at the airport runway. The Ramjet began moving slowly away from the boarding gate. As he watched, the stewards all seated themselves and clicked in their own restraints.

"Prepare for takeoff," the captain called again.

There was a surge of power as she increased thrust. The craft moved down the runway, gathering speed, pushing Tristan gently back into his well-padded seat. Then the nose rose, and the Ramjet left the ground.

Tristan was thrilled — this was the first time he'd ever been off the ground. He couldn't count when he'd fallen from the Worths' roof! The craft rose swiftly, and noises indicated when the landing gear had retracted and been sealed. Its nose raised, the ship gained altitude.

The view from the window was spectacular. It was late enough in the day for the city to be lit below him. Newark was a large city, and looked quite beautiful. To the east, though, was a black hole where the dazzling lights of New York should have been. Tristan felt a twinge of pain and guilt as he saw the gap. People were still trapped and dying there, while the lives of most people in the world — and out of it — simply went on as if nothing had happened.

The Ramjet rose higher and higher, and the sky became darker and darker. They passed through clouds, banking and turning out over the Atlantic Ocean as they climbed. There was little to see for the moment — ships and mining rigs were too small to be visible from this altitude, and the sea itself was pitch-dark. Still, one by one, the stars began to appear when the Ramjet cleared the top of the clouds. The FASTEN RESTRAINTS sign was still on and blinking, of course, because the main part of the thrust was still to come.

"Ten seconds to Ramjet ignition," the captain informed the passengers, and Tristan steeled himself. Escape velocity from Earth was 30 kilometers per second, far faster than any aircraft engine could manage. That was where the extra thrust of the Ramjet engine itself was needed — it would boost the speed of the shuttle up to the required level. But it couldn't be used too close to the ground, because of the sonic booms involved.

And then he felt the jets kick in. He was shoved back into his seat by the acceleration, and glad the seat was so padded. He had a moment's difficulty catching his breath, the pressure on his ribs being so great. Then he felt better, as the pressure began to ease. The acceleration died down, and the shuttle approached escape velocity.

Tristan glanced out of the window. They were rising much faster now, and the stars were coming out in all of their glory. In a few moments, they would have left Earth's atmosphere behind them and be on their way through space toward the waiting Overlook.

It was incredibly thrilling, and he was loving every second of it. It almost made him forget the dangerous nature of his mission.

Almost . . .

If the computers failed now, the ship would shut down. They would all die in orbit.

Shimoda was getting very, very scared. After more than a day of work, she was still no closer to an answer either for the guard dogs or the Doomsday Virus itself. Both were simply far too sophisticated for her to duplicate or destroy. She almost felt a grudging respect for the talents of Tristan Connor. If only he was on the side of good, instead of destruction!

She knew that she would never be able to crack this, and she didn't know what to do next. If she went to Chen to confess to failure, he'd probably assign someone else to try. Shimoda wasn't arrogant, but she knew she was the best in the department for this job — and if she couldn't do it, then nobody else would be able to manage it either. And if Chen were the traitor she suspected, he'd make sure an incompetent would be assigned.

And not stopping the virus would condemn millions to death or disaster. There *had* to be a way to stop it . . . only she didn't have a clue. What they needed was Tristan Connor. If anyone could stop this Armageddon-in-the-making, it was him. But nothing had turned up about his location. Shimoda wondered if Chen had done anything to expedite the boy's arrest, beyond the issuing of the Shield Priority Alert.

Since there was nothing she could do with the virus, Shimoda took a coffee break. She was exhausted. How long since she had last slept? She couldn't remember. But how could she sleep during this emergency? She'd never be able to forgive herself if the EarthNet was destroyed while she dozed. She just hoped the coffee would keep her alert enough to work. She logged in to the search data, and discovered that Chen had done nothing after alerting the police to pick up Connor on sight.

How *could* he have possibly overlooked the normal search procedures? He should have alerted all travel agencies, airports, ports, and flitter companies and sent them Connor's picture and ID logs! It was impossible that someone as efficient as Chen could simply forget to do this. . . .

Which meant he was *deliberately* obstructing the case. But why?

Was he one of Quietus's spies?

Now what? Shimoda could send out the alerts herself, and she was strongly tempted to do so. It was their best bet at catching Connor. Somehow, he'd managed to evade detection with his own IC. Maybe he'd found some sort of Identity-theft device, like the one Genia used? In which case, he'd be using somebody else's identity and funds to escape. Luckily he'd still *look* like Tristan Connor.

But . . . if Chen had deliberately obstructed that sort of search, he'd probably have some sort of a tag on the Net to let him know if anyone else issued one. In which case, he might override it and then take action directly against her.

After a bout of indecision, Shimoda copied the lack of data onto a disk and pocketed the small chip. She'd be able to prove that Chen had obstructed her, if that should become necessary in the future. But what to do next? Issue the alert, and probably set herself up as a target? But if she didn't, how could they catch Connor?

She was still agonizing over the choice when there was an incoming message for her. It was from a Lt. Barnes . . . oh, yes, Jill Barnes, one of the officers she'd worked with before. She hit ACCEPT, and Jill's face filled her Screen.

She was on a familiar-looking street, with the wreck of a flitter behind her, and a puzzled expression on her face. "Inspector," she said, "sorry to disturb you, but I've discovered something you might find of interest." She gestured over her shoulder. "A flitter crash not far from the home of Tristan Connor, the boy you're after. One of the corpses has been mutilated, and a second is . . . intriguing."

"Is it Connor?" Shimoda asked. Her stomach tied itself in knots. If the boy was dead, then disaster was imminent. On the other hand, if anyone deserved death more than Connor, she couldn't imagine who.

"No." Barnes frowned. "Remember ordering a DNA check on a suspect a while back?"

Of course she did; it had ended up belonging to Borden, a ninety-year-old member of Computer Control — but it had been taken from a young man. "The one that got mixed up with Borden's DNA?" she asked.

"It wasn't mixed up," Barnes informed her. "This corpse *is* Borden — at least, it has his DNA, all right. But it's a young man in his twenties."

Shimoda stared at the Screen in amazement. "So the man *was* a clone . . ." she breathed. Cloning living people was completely illegal, of course. But it was obvious that the people involved in this case weren't bothered by such minor matters. "Barnes, get that body to the morgue as fast as possible. And for your own sake, don't tell anybody else about this. Get the body sealed away, and lose the official report on it. There's at least one traitor in our department, and it might even be Chen himself. If they know what you've discovered, your life may be in danger."

Jill's face paled. "It's that bad?"

"It's that bad." Shimoda was about to wish her friend luck and sign off when the rest of her report sank in. "The mutilated man," she said. "*How* was he mutilated?"

"His wrist was almost severed, and his IC removed."

Shimoda felt a sense of absolute certainty. These were the men who had attacked Connor before, and they were now dead. She *knew* Connor had to be involved. And now she knew why they hadn't been able to find Connor. . . . He had the dead man's IC, and was using his account. "Do we have identification on the corpse?" she demanded.

"We don't have identification on any of the corpses," Barnes answered. "I can't scan the two remaining IC readings at all. I doubt we'd do better on the third. Somehow they're blocked to scans."

"Blast," Shimoda muttered. So close . . . but if they couldn't scan Tristan, he was effectively invisible to them. And the existence of such chips proved that there was high-powered help for Quietus somewhere — and then a thought struck her. "Jill, get me a scan of the mutilated man's DNA and send it to me." At least Quietus couldn't blank *that* out. "Then get all three bodies to the morgue and lose the whole report on them. Don't talk to *anyone* else at all about this."

"Right."

Shimoda waited, her excitement growing. Maybe they did have a way to track Connor, after all. . . .

The data she wanted came through. Quickly, she copied the DNA scan and sent queries out to the Net, to see if anyone with that DNA had made any recent purchases. It would take a little while to get the reply, and she used that time to "lose" the call from Barnes. It was getting scary, having to hide what she knew like this. But she had no option, until she was certain exactly who in the department she could trust.

And then the answer came through: The man had bought a ticket on the Delta's shuttle flight to Overlook!

"He's trying to get out of my jurisdiction," Shimoda muttered. If he got to another planet, then Shimoda would have to request extradition. That would be a political matter, and might take months. On the other hand, Overlook was still within her legal limits.

If she could capture him there.

Urgently, she put a call through to the garage and ordered a Ramjet readied for her as quickly as possible. Connor's flight had taken off an hour ago, which meant he'd reach Overlook in about five hours. The shield ship was faster than the commercial one. The garage informed her it would be ready in thirty minutes. She could be on her way fast enough to reach Overlook an hour after Connor. She checked for connecting flights off the station again, and there weren't any until six hours after the Delta's arrival.

She'd find him there.

Of course, what she *should* do was call Overlook's own shield department and have them arrest Connor as he arrived. But she didn't know if they were in on the conspiracy, too. She needed someone whom she could trust to back her up, and that meant handpicking her team. And quickly . . .

But at least she now knew she could have Connor. And she *would* have him.

After all, he could hardly escape her in the confines of Overlook, could he?

He was trapped now.

10

Despite the urgency of his mission, Tristan couldn't help enjoying his flight. As soon as Earth had been left behind, gravity diminished. Only the restraints had kept Tristan from floating away. Like a number of the other passengers, he'd deliberately loosened the belts so that he floated several inches off his chair. It felt really weird but wonderful, and he wished he had the time to take it all in. But he didn't. He dozed during the flight, despite the excitement, because he knew he'd need to be fresh to confront Devon and stop the virus.

He awoke again as preparations were being made for docking. Startled, he looked out of his window and saw an astonishing sight.

Against the blackness of the sky and the untwinkling stars, he could see Overlook. It was a flattened sphere, with nine starfishlike arms, ending in further spheres. It wasn't symmetrical, giving it a sort of lopsided appearance. It was lit up, and there was a horde of small ships clustered or moving about it. Attached to one of the docking ports was a deep-space ship, a long, flat craft with nuclear engines at the rear.

It was impossible to get any real idea of the size of the place, except that it was constantly growing. It virtually filled the window as Tristan looked out, and the shuttle moved in closer. From time to time, Tristan heard the quiet venting of a correcting rocket engine as the shuttle edged in closer and closer.

Overlook had to be over a mile across, Tristan realized with awe. By now he could see only a quarter of the place. The shuttle gently moved toward a docking bay close to the deep-space ship. In the open bay, lights blinked as targets. Beside the bay were windows, and controllers were watching the shuttle's approach.

Finally, the shuttle's docking port was in position,

and Tristan heard the clamps from the docking bay snap out and latch firmly onto the shuttle.

"This is Captain O'Hara," came the woman's voice over the Screens. "Please remain in your seats until docking is completed. The stewards will inform you when you may leave your seats and enter Overlook. Thank you all for flying Delta, and we hope you will select us as your carrier for any further flights. Have a wonderful day — if you can tell day from night in space!"

Tristan obeyed the instructions, not wanting to draw attention to himself, though some of the other passengers started moving around. Probably the old hands at space travel, Tristan realized. Gravity of sorts had returned — not real gravity and not terribly strong. It was a force produced by the rotation of Overlook, with the strange effect that "down" was toward the side of the shuttle away from the station — in this case, the right-hand wall. Tristan felt as if he were lying on his side, though he was sitting down.

One of the stewards approached him. "Have you ever been in space before?" the man asked. When Tristan confessed he hadn't, the man smiled reassuringly. "You'll get used to it," he promised. "The trick is to move slowly, because any movements you make in microgravity will have much bigger results than they would in normal gravity. You'll probably hit your head on the ceiling a few times before you get the hang of it, but it's amazing how fast a couple of bruises speed up the learning process. Now" — he leaned over Tristan — "I'm going to release your restraints. When I do, swing around and let yourself drop toward me. Flex your knees, and bend them to absorb the impact. Don't push down, or you'll launch yourself like a rocket. Okay."

The straps came free, and Tristan swung around, letting his feet drop toward the wall that was now the floor. He landed with surprising gentleness.

"That's it," the steward said approvingly, handing Tristan his pack. "Be slow and gentle, and you'll be fine. And if you need help, ask."

Tristan thanked the man and walked very gingerly toward the docking port. Each step made it seem like he was floating, but he made it without hitting his head on anything. Then he was out the exit, past smiling stewardesses, and into Overlook itself.

There was a short docking tunnel into the station. The main area looked like a roundabout, moving in a circle. The approach was across several strips, each getting slightly faster as Tristan proceeded. As he moved forward, his "weight" increased, thanks to the spinning force pushing him down toward the "floor." By the time he reached the station itself, he weighed almost half as much as he would on Earth, so he felt a lot more comfortable.

He left the area, heading toward the duty-free shops. The first thing he needed was a good hand-comp, and this was the best place to get one. Most were manufactured on Overlook or one of the other stations anyway, so they were relatively cheap, even for top-of-the-line models. Not that he was exactly bothered about a budget right now. He picked one of the more expensive ones, and paid for it with the stolen IC. Then he downloaded a map of Overlook and checked his Centrus account. The guard dogs were still holding off the virus, thankfully, but he could tell that they were weakening. There wasn't much time before they failed completely.

On the map, Tristan located Devon's rooms. Then, following the large signs on the walls, he made his way toward them.

The station was huge, and busy. Tristan had never seen so many real people in any place before. There had to be dozens in every corridor, all with places to go, things to do, and other people to meet. He wondered if people bothered using Virtual Reality here, or whether they were hardy souls who actually traveled places on their feet.

Other than the crowds, though, the place resembled .comshops and NetMalls, so he didn't feel too out of his depth. He'd traveled similar buildings before, even if they didn't really exist. As he approached the residential sector, the crowds thinned out. Finally, he was the only one in the corridor leading toward Devon's quarters.

It was the perfect place for an ambush, if that was what Devon had in mind. But what could Tristan do about it? He had no choice but to go on, his eyes and ears open for any sign of a trap.

There was something in the corridor ahead of him. Cautiously, he approached it, and stared in puzzlement. It was a Housebot, but something had torn its head off. A short way farther on was a 'bot that had been fried with a staser. What had happened here? It looked like there had been a fight.

Had someone already tracked down Devon? The shields, maybe? Was his trip here for nothing? No, that couldn't be it — the virus was still loose, so he'd have to shut it down, no matter what had happened.

Tristan reached the door to Devon's rooms. Now

what? He used his hand-comp to hook into the entry panel. It was code-locked, of course, but that wasn't any problem. Removing his glove, Tristan let the panel sample his DNA. Since it matched Devon's exactly, the computer was expecting Devon's code to be entered. Using a quick burst of code, Tristan fooled the computer into thinking the password had been given, and noted what the machine registered.

He now had Devon's operating code for his rooms. Perfect.

The door slid open, and Tristan paused, listening. There was no sound from within. Tristan used the hand-comp once again to query the housekeeping computer for Devon's location. It showed that he wasn't in the rooms at all.

Maybe he'd just popped out to buy something? In which case, Tristan might have the time to do what he needed, or else he could be interrupted any time. He left a command to be alerted if anyone else opened the door, and then went into Devon's world.

It was astonishingly luxurious. Tristan's father was the vice president of a bank, and made good money, so Tristan was used to a good lifestyle. But this place was furnished for a billionaire. Real paintings adorned the walls, and thick, luxurious carpets covered the floors.

There was real wooden furniture, which must have been incredibly expensive to ship into space. The bedroom was large, and there was even a private swimming pool.

But it was the office that Tristan was after, and there he stood, staring, for several minutes.

The room had one wall filled with Screens. When he powered up the Terminal, they came to life, each showing different pictures. Devon used the room to watch the world, it seemed. Some were street scenes, others inside buildings. One screen even showed a girl hooked into Virtual Reality. Devon was spying on people — a peeping tom! What a creep!

The computer equipment in here was magnificent — state of the art, the best money could buy. Multiple processors, surround VR, the works. Tristan was impressed. He immediately logged on, using the code he'd stolen from the door.

"Ready," said a gentle voice from the air, about two feet above his head. Verbal command, obviously. It could be quick, but Tristan preferred to use the speedboard. He grabbed it and started hunting for the virus generator.

"I knew you'd be back, Devon!"

Tristan spun around in the soft chair he'd taken over.

Facing him was an eight-foot figure, a black smoky wraith. He didn't have a clue who or what it was, but it had clearly, understandably, mistaken him for Devon. He had no intention of correcting the mistake. If only he could keep the person thinking he was his own clone!

"What do you want?" he asked, figuring that to be a safe question. He couldn't exactly ask the person who he was, because Devon would obviously know.

"Arrogant as ever," the wraith snarled. "Don't forget that *I* made you what you are, Devon, and I can unmake you. And I didn't call myself the Malefactor for no reason."

Now he knew who this person was, sort of. He was an on-line personality, invented by the real person cloaked in the blackness, of course, but at least it was a start. Tristan started a query into "Malefactor" in Devon's files.

"What do you want?" Tristan repeated. He had nothing to fear from a projection, and if he got Devon into trouble, so much the better.

"I want you to download the virus parameters," the Malefactor answered. "I must be able to recreate the virus in case the stupid policewoman on the case does manage to stop your release. I cannot allow the plans of Quietus to be brought to a halt because of your foolishness."

"*My* foolishness?" Tristan asked. The Malefactor had said Devon was arrogant, and Tristan had guessed that from his own contact with the boy. "I'm the one who created the virus, don't forget."

"And don't forget that you can be punished!" the Malefactor snapped. "Do as I say. Quietus *must* have the virus to complete our plans."

Tristan realized that their whole scheme was clearly more than simply Devon being crazy enough to create and release the Doomsday Virus. This Quietus group had a plan, and the virus was a key part of it. But, so far, only Devon had control over it. And the Malefactor obviously no longer trusted Devon. There was no way, of course, that Tristan could even think of giving the virus to such people. And, probably, neither would Devon. So the answer was obvious. "Get stuffed," Tristan snapped.

And his search engine found the generator! He had discovered the point of origin for the virus! Now all he needed was the time to destroy it from within.

"I expected as much," the Malefactor replied. "Devon, do you think I would be foolish enough to give you unlimited power without retaining some control over you?" The face of the wraith was not visible, but Tristan could hear the triumph in the voice alone.

Then his whole body spasmed in agony. He knew absolutely nothing but pain for several seconds. Then it stopped. Gradually, Tristan could move and feel and think again. The blinding spots vanished from in front of his eyes, and his fingers unclenched. He'd managed to score his palm with his nails, leaving bloody trails.

"That was just a sample of the pain I can deliver," the Malefactor gloated. "Your chair has been wired to feed electrical currents directly into the pain control center of your brain. Next time, I will leave you under for ten seconds. Twice the agony . . . " He paused to let this terrible thought sink in. "Now — transmit the parameters of the virus, so that I can recreate it."

The man was a monster. Tristan could still barely move. But he couldn't let this man gain control of the virus. On the other hand . . . He checked the speedboard and discovered that there was a link to an outside account — the one he was supposed to send the data to.

Instead, Tristan created a link directly to the virus generator.

"I'll do better than that," he informed the Malefactor. "I'll give you the virus itself."

"No!" the wraith screamed, but it was too late. Tristan had downloaded the virus into the other man's machine. He'd also managed to add a time limit to the codes, so the virus would destroy itself in five seconds. Long enough to wipe out the Malefactor's computer, but not long enough to escape again into the Net. The projection of the madman exploded, and the link was severed as the virus ate up the Malefactor's machine.

Sweating with relief and shock, Tristan bent back to work. His guard dogs were terribly weak now, and might fail any second. He typed commands feverishly, isolating the virus generator, and then turning it on itself. If his plan worked, the virus would stop consuming outside codes to grow with and instead feed only off itself, wiping itself out.

As he worked, the door chimed, warning him that somebody else was entering the apartment. Tristan cursed — of all the times for Devon to return! But he couldn't stop now. If he didn't finish his command codes, the virus would be unstoppable. He focused on the task, ignoring everything else.

The guard dogs collapsed, and the virus was poised to escape and destroy all of the Net.

Tristan tapped the "transmit" code, and watched, terrified he'd made a mistake.

For a second that stretched into eternity, nothing seemed to happen.

And then the virus began folding back, consuming itself. It ravaged backward, through the New York computers, leaving nothing in its dead wake. It ate up all of the virus, and returned to the generator in Devon's computers. There it ravaged all of the data before Tristan could stop it. But he had isolated the virus into the one machine. And there was only one thing he could do.

He destroyed Devon's Terminal. Using the handcomp, he simply annihilated the memory banks. He was losing his best chance to find out what Devon and Quietus were up to, but he didn't care. He *had* to destroy the virus, utterly.

The room went dark as the Screens all died. The speedboard shut down; the projectors ceased.

Alone in the dark, Tristan stumbled to the door. He'd left the house-comp isolated, so he should be able to get out of here, at least. To face his lethal clone. Tristan took a deep breath and triggered the door . . .

To stare into two stasers aimed directly for him. Behind one stood Inspector Shimoda. Behind the second, another shield woman he didn't recognize.

"Tristan Connor," Inspector Shimoda said grimly.

"You're under arrest. And I really hope to God you try to resist. Because there's nothing I'd love more right now than to beat you to a pulp."

"You don't understand," Tristan exclaimed. "I'm not the person you want. It's my clone, Devon. *He* created the virus! I just shut it down and saved the Net. Check it for yourself."

Shimoda didn't lower her weapon, but she moved her wrist-comp so she could check it. Her eyes widened. "The virus *is* gone."

"I told you." Tristan started to breathe a little easier. It looked like she was being reasonable. "I stopped it."

"You expect thanks for that?" Shimoda smiled tightly. "Just because you stopped your little scheme when you were about to be arrested will avail you nothing. Maybe get a year knocked off your sentence." She gestured with her weapon. "Come out here, Connor. You're under arrest and, I promise you, you are going to be Iced for the rest of your miserable, stinking life."

Tristan stared at her in horror. He'd told her the truth, and she didn't believe him. Now what could he do? When the staser moved menacingly, he knew.

He went forward. The second officer used a force bar on his wrists to immobilize him. Helpless, he stood by as Shimoda used her wrist-comp. "Get the ship ready for immediate departure," she ordered. "We're bringing the scum in for justice."

Justice? Tristan knew that was the last thing he'd get. Instead, he was about to be punished for all of Devon's crimes, while his clone went free. He didn't even try to argue. It was clear that Shimoda didn't believe that Tristan was innocent.

Would anyone?

TO BE CONTINUED IN:

2099

traitor